An Empty Vessel

An Empty Vessel

Evelyn M. Cowan

iUniverse, Inc.
Bloomington

An Empty Vessel

iUniverse books may be ordered through booksellers or by contacting:

iUniverse
1663 Liberty Drive
Bloomington, IN 47403
www.iuniverse.com
1-800-Authors (1-800-288-4677)

ISBN: 978-1-4620-3885-5 (sc)
ISBN: 978-1-4620-3886-2 (ebk)

Printed in the United States of America

iUniverse rev. date: 07/13/2011

Dedicated to my well beloved Bernard,
who has made heaven on high
his home. Yet, he is ever with me.

Prologue

This memoir is the result of several years of a commitment to impart my unbelievable saga to the universe. The legend is the offspring of my fervent labor of love.

It is the true and poignant narrative of a woman with emotional illness, named India, who becomes homeless in the fifth month of her pregnancy.

She was transcended from the height of ecstasy to the depths of despair when her newborn blessing is snatched from her breast like a lovely flower, plucked up from its roots, and placed in foster care.

What follows is a heartfelt account of how she overcomes unspeakable trials and tribulations, and how her unyielding faith in God ultimately sustains, and carries her from glory to glory.

She is eventually reunited with her only child, but only after they both suffer deep, invisible scars which would remain throughout their lifetimes.

India receives some divine recompense when she, at last, comes into her undeniable destiny.

Chapter One

There shall not be found among you any one
That maketh his son or his daughter to pass through the fire . . .
Deuteronomy 18:10

India Crown wasn't sure exactly what had caused the schism in her mind. She didn't know if, perhaps, it had been something lurking in her genealogy, or if it had been generated by the years of dwelling with an oppressive, overbearing mother. Perchance the latter had triggered the former, and kindled what emerged as a mental breakdown.

India's mother harbored a vehement distain for her which she had never understood growing up, and doubted that she ever could. When she was only twelve years old, her mother had taken out a life insurance policy on India, who later concluded that it was her mother's secret desire that she would never reach adulthood. But she did, despite the odds. And she was twenty years old when she slipped into a deep depression.

She locked herself into her bedroom, and refused to eat anything or get out of her bed. After three days, her mother called the law. The responding officers busted down India's bedroom door, and attempted her to coax her into rendering some kind of response. But they were unable to penetrate the invisible wall which she had subconsciously constructed as a defense mechanism in a futile effort to allay her inward anguish.

"What's going on India?" asked one of the officers.

India remained silent and still.

"Tell us how we can help you," he urged.

When India failed to reply, her mother interjected, "She's been like this for days. I didn't know what else to do," she lamented with feigned concern.

Eventually, an ambulance was summoned to transport India to a psychiatric hospital for evaluation. That was the first of numerous hospitalizations of which her mother availed herself whenever she wanted India removed from her presence.

India had always shared a strange love/hate relationship with her mother. And her spirit was quite fragile from being used as her mother's personal scapegoat, blamed for everything that went wrong in their home life.

Her father had died when India was seven years old, leaving her and her brother, Craig, alone to fend for themselves against a matriarch who had always placed her career ambitions ahead of them. Their mother would leave before them each morning enroute to work, and then school. So they readied themselves and trotted off to school, and then returned to an empty house each afternoon, as their mother pursued various degrees. They learned to depend on each other.

But, Craig left home after graduating from high school, moving from their home in California to Phoenix, Arizona to embark on a life of his own. India, however, had a difficult, if not impossible time escaping the symbiotic ties which bound her to her tyrannical mother. So she remained, playing the martyr, and bearing the burden and the blame. And endured suffering all of the damning negativity that was constantly heaped upon her. She silently recoiled from life as a result of the many years and tears of criticism and cruelty.

India's mother made no effort to hide the fact that she wanted her out of her house and out of her life completely. Once, India had loaned her $300. And when she made no effort to repay her, India timidly asked her mother when she intended to reimburse her for the loan. "I'll hand it to you as you are walking out my door for good," she snarled.

"But you promised to repay me promptly," India reminded her.

"I'm not about to keep supporting some grown, rusty woman," her mother retorted. India just shook her head in silent surrender, and succumbed to her mother's illogical outrage. She retreated, in defeat, to the still seclusion of her room, where she concluded that she must seek employment. It was the only way to break free from the depressing dependency upon her mother, and arise to the possibilities of sustaining herself.

India began searching for a job the very next day. And she didn't relent until she secured a position as a teacher's aide at an elementary school for the San Gabriel School District. Although her pay was meager, India thoroughly enjoyed interacting with the young children, and took great pride in her newfound autonomy. She had to leave early in order to catch two buses to work, but the commute to the neighboring community—provided her with no time to reflect on her life, and how she might reconstruct her chaotic circumstances.

One October day, as she was walking home from the bus stop, lost in her thoughts, she was scarcely aware of the brown Mustang pulling up alongside her. "Do you want a ride?" the occupant addressed her, "I know where you live." India turned, and her eyes caught his enticing countenance. What a pretty black boy, she thought. His curly black hair was to his shoulders. His smile was most inviting, enveloping her. "I want to see if you know where I live", challenged India as she walked toward the car, as if drawn by some inevitable energy. "What's your name?" asked India as she settled into her seat. "Bernard", he replied. Of course, it couldn't be anything else, she thought, as he rounded the corner and stopped in front of India's house.

She thanked him for the lift, and added that she hoped to see him again. That brief encounter laid the foundation for what would be the most vital and essential relationship of India's life.

Clearly Bernard also perceived that their first encounter was an appointment with destiny because later that day India returned home from visiting and elderly neighbor to find Bernard standing at her front door. She invited him inside, and they sat on the couch and acquainted themselves with one another. India discovered that Bernard lived merely a few blocks away. By the time he left, hours later, she had invited him to dinner that Sunday, and they both heartily concluded that their meeting had been kismet.

After bidding Bernard farewell, India leaned against the door, lingering on each moment that they had spent together, and, from that instant, she was under his spell.

Chapter Two

I am my beloved's and my beloved is mine:
He feedeth among the lilies.
Song of Solomon 6:3

As the seasons followed, India and Bernard's magnetism flourished into a tangible love. A decade came and went. It was Christmastide, 1988.

India awakened and slowly rolled over in bed. Could she still be dreaming? No, he was right there beside her, asleep. She studied his perfect, chocolate colored face, and suddenly, all of the warm embers, still smoldering from last night's passion, burned in her mind. For the past ten years, there had been no one else but him. From the very second when they first met, India had adored him. And though he rarely spoke it, she knew that Bernard loved her too. True, he hadn't always been there for her, sometimes even staying away for months at a time. But she was always there for him, waiting in the wings. And now she was pregnant. It was something they had both secretly wished for from the beginning, and India now felt that they had finally been blessed. As she fondly recalled the torrid love they'd made the night before, Bernard awakened.

"Good morning, Love", she whispered. He kissed her tenderly, and didn't stop until they were making love again. Afterwards, Bernard got up and sat down on the wicker chair beside the bed. He gazed at India's naked body as she lay, still, on the bed.

"Do you remember the first time we met?" he asked.

"Yes. I was walking home from the bus stop, coming from work, when you pulled up alongside me and asked if I wanted a ride. You claimed you knew where I lived." India felt nostalgic as she recounted their first encounter. "I took you home didn't I?" Bernard paused for a moment. "Do you remember the first time we did it?" he persisted. India smiled. "My mother was out of town, and I had just gotten my new water bed, and we christened it."

They both were silent for a moment, remembering, as they communicated their joy in the unspoken language that so often conveyed their innermost feelings. Suddenly, India arose and straddled Bernard. She hugged him tightly as he asked, "India, do you want to do it again"?

"Yes", she sighed.

"Do you want to do it right here, or on the bed?" he inquired.

"On the bed", she responded as she glided back onto the twin bed which was nowhere big enough for their insatiable antics. Their love had taken on a new meaning and dimension ever since they had learned about the pregnancy. It had a sense of fulfillment and joy which had not been there before.

Usually, in the afterglow, he would rest his body upon hers, with his head upon her breast, like a pillow. But now, he almost immediately rose up off of her protruding abdomen, and lay beside her. "Are you hungry?" she asked. "A little", he replied. So India raised herself out of bed and adorned her robe. She began to prepare a B.L.T. And, as she was frying the bacon, she noticed that Bernard was now standing and staring at her, the look of love lighting up his entire face. He had simply thrilled at the news of her pregnancy, and, although she was merely two months along, he just knew that the baby was a girl. He'd say things like, "I bet she's going to be so cute," and "If she's bad, I'm going to whip her." To which India had responded, "You'd better not lay a hand on that child!" He would just smile that coy smile of his.

After he gobbled down the B.L.T., he dressed and left, saying he would be back alter. India got in the shower and gingerly massaged the small lump in her growing belly with the soapy washcloth, while reveling in the warm water streaming down her body. She lingered longer than usual, letting the water flow down her back, as she thought about Bernard. She knew that there had been many other women and that he had been unwilling to commit to her, although he knew that he was the only man in her life, the only man she desired. Perhaps that's why he'd never married her in their ten years apart and together. Because he knew that she was unconditionally his.

But things had definitely changed since he found out about the baby. He had definitely changed. When he left, like he did that morning, saying that he would be back later, he always returned. Before, she might not see him again for months. He would pick her lovely pink flowers from outside in the yard, and present them to her, beaming. He seemed to do whatever he could to make her happy. And she was. Because things were becoming the way India had always wanted them to be, and she and Bernard were closer than they had ever been.

The pregnancy was a miracle in itself. After all, she was 32 years old, four years his senior, and this was her second pregnancy. The first had ended tragically in a miscarriage when India was sixteen years old. Her mother, preoccupied with her own life and oblivious to India's, had known nothing of it. And India was relieved when, after about fourteen weeks, the pregnancy abruptly ended, along with her first love affair. Because of the secret, she had not sought medical attention, and had flushed the embryo down the toilet, where she had miscarried.

Later, after years of trying unsuccessfully to conceive, she regretfully concluded that she was barren. She had longed for a baby for so long, particularly Bernard's baby, but hadn't thought it was possible. India had even endured false pregnancies, where she'd convinced herself that she was pregnant. Those phantom pregnancies always culminated in anguished sorrow, after India was forced to come to terms with the fact that her profound yearning for a child was merely a pipe dream. Once, India, so adamant in her dubious quest, actually went into labor. The pain was real, but incomparable to that of having to mourn what, in all actuality, was a fleeting fantasy.

But now, she felt exceedingly blessed, and that baby she was carrying was a divine manifestation of God's grace, goodness and glory, because he had finally answered her fervent prayers. She emerged from the shower feeling content and consoled that Bernard and her love had finally come into fruition. As she was dressing, the telephone rang. It was him.

"How's my baby?" he inquired.

"Which one?" teased India.

"Both of you", he replied and then added, "I miss you."

"You just left an hour ago", laughed India.

"I'll see you in a while", promised Bernard.

Later that evening, Bernard returned to his brother, Tony, and one of their friends. India knew what this meant. Soon after they had sat down in the small, one room apartment that India called home, they brought out the crack pipe. India did not know exactly when Bernard had started this dreadful habit, but she knew that it had caused him to lose his job after he had been caught embezzling money from the bank he had worked at since graduating from high school. He had somehow managed to avoid jail time, but he had been unable to secure another job. And not only could he not help her financially, but he had actually stolen money from her purse.

India watched as they passed the pipe to one another, taking turns, inhaling the white rocks, which would disintegrate into smoke inside of the glass vessel. In between hits, they talked about different things, and India would join in the conversation, but never did she partake of their poisonous pastime. Cocaine had been responsible for killing at least three of her close friends since high school, and she was deathly afraid of the drug in any form.

India had never attempted to dissuade Bernard from the pipe. She sensed that it would do no good anyway, so she simply chose to keep silent about the fact that his life was literally going up in smoke. And she had become an enabler. Not only did she say nothing, but she provided them with a safe haven to engage in their deadly get togethers.

After awhile, Tony and his friend left, leaving Bernard and India alone. It was now almost nighttime, and India decided to light a candle to vanquish the approaching darkness. She removed an old, burned out candle from the candleholder and placed it in the top drawer of her desk, before lighting a new, white candle. The drawer contained a dozen or more small, burned out candles.

"What are you saving these for?" inquired Bernard.

"So you can make me a candle with them," India offered with a smile. His face lit up in the soft glow of the candlelight. "Oh, I'm going to make you a candle . . . I'm going to make you the most beautiful candle . . . I'm going to make you a candle . . .," he murmured. He was surprised that she remembered him telling her, when they had met ten years prior, that he used to make candles, as a child, when he was an altar boy. India gazed sternly at Bernard. His eyes were glossy, and he seemed to be somewhere far, far away.

"I want to give you your Christmas present," she exclaimed. His lethargy turned quickly into anticipation. "But Christmas isn't until tomorrow!" Ignoring him, she reached into a cabinet and brought forth a gift, wrapped with tissue paper and ribbon. "It's a hat," he said, taking the gift. It was obvious. There had been no way to conceal the shape of the baseball cap. "Open it," she ordered. He ripped the paper off and smiled broadly when he saw the Playboy emblem on the front of the cap. "I love it!" he exclaimed. India had meant for it to be a sarcastic gesture, but he failed to get the point. And as he looked in the mirror, and adjusted it so that it fit just so, she thought, "Oh well, so much for sarcasm." She was glad that he liked it so much, and it really did look good on him.

It was a wonderful Christmas that year. Bernard spent the day and night with her, and India prepared a special dinner with all of his favorite things just for the two of them in her little place that had become a love nest for them. She prayed that thing would always be this way between them, and that if all her prayers were answered, they would marry before the baby came.

Chapter Three

Remember, O Lord, what is come upon us:
Consider and behold our reproach.
Lamentations 5:1

But there was an ill wind blowing, and things soon turned from bittersweet to disastrous. One morning, Bernard came over at about 2:00 am. India could tell that he was high and he had also been drinking. Apparently, all of his guilt feelings had gotten the best of him, and he felt compelled to confess to India about all of the other women, and affairs he had engaged in when he had not been with her. That was the last thing she wanted to hear, especially now, with her hormone raging from the pregnancy. She wished he would just keep his old skeletons in the closet, and in the past, where they belonged. But he proceeded to clear his conscience in spite of her protests.

So India listened, silently growing more and more angry, as Bernard undauntedly went on and on about all of his past lovers. When he was finished, she'd asked him to leave and then, cried herself to sleep.

Logic played no part in the rage India felt. Her delicate condition, coupled with the fact that all of her feelings of betrayal over the past ten years had just been validated, left no room for logic. And she could not see beyond the hurt. She was unable to comprehend at the time that perhaps the reason Bernard had chosen to bear his soul now was because he did not want to marry her. And he had not wanted to carry all of his excess baggage into their union.

Over the next few weeks India went about her everyday life in a sort of a daze, performing her tasks in a robot-like manner, as her mind and thoughts strayed far from the chores and activities she attempted. Once, in the middle of the night, he had come around to the side window, and had tapped on it relentlessly, saying, “India, I got you a watch.” “Give it to Emily,” she had replied. Emily was atop his list of lovers.

“I have some things for the baby,” he’d answered. India ignored him. It was raining outside, and she wondered how long he would stand there in the rain.

Suddenly, she leapt to her feet, and went to the door and flung it open. She called to him, but he had gone, and it would be several months before she would see him again. During that time, something happened for which India was totally unprepared, that would forever change the course of her life. Before moving to her apartment, India resided at a Board and Care Home for people that suffered from a variety of emotional and mental illnesses. And she had grown stronger since residing at the Board and Care facility. When she looked in the mirror, she now saw the loving, caring, vital person that she was and she was surrounded by sensitive people who saw her in like manner.

She hadn’t seen Bernard as often in the two years of her convalescence, but sometimes he would call and ask her to meet him at his parent’s house, a few blocks away. They owned a beautiful two story home, with a small guest house in the back, where she and Bernard would rendezvous and make passionate love. It was there that India conceived, much to her amazement.

When the doctor had confirmed her pregnancy, India left his office ecstatic and astonished. She knew she had to move, and immediately began searching for a place that she could afford. She received Supplemental Social Security Income for her disability, as did all of the residents of the Board and Care facility. It paid for their room and board, plus a small stipend for their personal needs. But now she needed to explore independent living, with a baby on the horizon.

India soon found an apartment within her budget, and moved in immediately. It was tiny, yet kind of quaint, and rather charming. She had not yet informed Bernard of the pregnancy, and decided to write him a letter. That way, she could say all she needed to express to him without him interrupting. And she’d poured her heart out in the letter, summing up just how deeply her feelings ran.

When he received the letter, he’d phoned her immediately. When she answered the phone, he said, “Prince, I’ll be right over.”

“Who is this?” asked India, thinking it was the wrong number.

"Bernard," he answered.

India gasped, and realized that he was referring to the baby as "Prince."

He had been overcome with joy, and their lives were blissful until his "true confessions."

The manager of the apartment building was a young, handsome, Jewish man named Billy. He was obviously taken aback by the fact that India was oblivious to his good looks and indifferent to his advances. She had dealt with his type of arrogance before but never had the offender been her manager. She told him that she was pregnant, but that just seemed to encourage him further. She had hoped that he would not cause any problems for her, because it would be difficult, if not impossible, to find another place that she could afford. She knew that the situation could escalate into a case of sexual harassment if Billy decided to become vindictive simply because his inflated ego had been bruised. And that is precisely what happened.

On the first of February, India went to the mailbox to retrieve her S.S.I. check, which always arrived, like clockwork, on the first of each month. Her heart sank, when to her surprise it was not there. Later, she surmised that Billy could have actually removed it, but, at the time, she didn't know that he was as cold blooded as he would prove to be. India tried not to panic. She returned to her apartment, and immediately called the toll-free number for the Social Security office to inquire about the matter. They told her that her check had been mailed to her address on schedule, but, if it failed to arrive in the morrow, to report to the local Social Security office that she had not received it, and they would re-issue her another check.

The next morning she anxiously awaited the postman's arrival, and rushed to the mailbox as soon as he delivered the mail. But her hopes were dashed when she opened the empty box. So she started on the long trek to the Social Security office. Before she got out of the driveway, Billy pulled up in his truck.

He stopped and rolled down the window, and proceeded to question her, "I see you didn't pay your rent yesterday," Billy remarked.

"My check didn't come," India explained. "I was just on my way to the Social Security Office to inquire about it."

Billy just stared at her with a look of scorn on his face.

"I'll let you know what happens, okay?" India offered as she walked away.

At the Social Security office, India was told that it would take approximately fourteen days to reissue another check. She didn't worry too much, because she thought she had until the first of the next month to pay back her rent without the fear of eviction. But, to her shock and disbelief, Billy issued an eviction notice only a few days later. Not knowing where to turn or what else to do, she packed up all of her belonging, having absolutely no idea where she was going. She could not believe that this was actually happening to her. She tried to reason with Billy, but to no avail.

And on the appointed day of the eviction, he arrived with two marshals. They could see that India was obviously pregnant, and they entered the dwelling and saw that she had all of her possessions neatly packed up. The marshals then left, admonishing Billy and India to try to work things out. However, Billy then took matters into his own hands. He gathered up all of her things, packed them onto the back of his truck, and hauled them away, taking the key to her apartment before he left. India was literally left out in the cold. She was sure that this was illegal, not only in the manner in which she had been evicted, but also the fact that he had just stolen everything that she owned. Could this be some sort of ploy of Billy's to whisk her into his life? She didn't know. The only thing that was certain was that she was nearly five months pregnant and homeless.

India was adamant about not calling Bernard. There was nothing that he could do anyway, as he was staying with his parents, and her living with them was out of the question. Bernard's mother hated India for her obsession with him over the years, especially when he would be nowhere around. She would call incessantly, and the relentlessness of India's desire for her youngest child, her baby boy, had left Bernard's mother cold toward her, to say the least.

And turning to her own mother for help was another impossibility. They were estranged, and her mother even had a Restraining Order on India, forbidding her to set foot on her property. It seemed that after she'd tired of having her put in mental hospitals simply because she did not want her around, and could no longer deal with her problems, she had banned India from her home, and her life, wanting nothing whatsoever to do with her.

India had never felt so all alone. She decided to walk to the realty office and try to talk to the owner. After all, Billy was merely the manager. When she got there, she found the boxes containing all of her belongings, sitting on the front porch. Inside the office was Billy, sitting behind a desk, with his feet propped up, looking quite proud of himself.

"I'd like to speak to Mr. Clark," India started, "because I know enough about the law to know that you illegally took possession of my things," she continued.

"He's not available," Billy chided, avoiding India's fixed gaze.

"You were supposed to set everything outside of the apartment for me to do with whatever I wanted," India explained. When Billy ignored her, India left to go call the police.

An officer soon arrived, and India explained to him what had transpired, as she fought back tears. The officer was very sympathetic and went inside to speak to Billy, who presented him with a sheet of paper. It was a bogus list of supposed damages incurred at the apartment. They were a bunch of lies. India wanted to scream. The officer told her that she was free to take her things. But she had no way to transport the large boxes, so she gathered a few clothes in a pillowcase, and left.

In the days that followed, India wandered aimlessly around the city. She went back to the apartment, and tried to rest on an old loveseat that was outside, in the backyard. But Billy came with his truck and took that away, saying nothing. She wondered how anyone could be so cruel. Finally, she relocated up to her mother's neighborhood, and sought shelter in one of her neighbor's old cards which was parked in their driveway. When night fell upon her like a bandit, robbing her of any security that was afforded by the light of day, the car offered shelter. It was parked close to the neighbor's house, not far from her mother's house, and India would stealthily enter it late at night after the occupants of the house had turned off their lights and gone to bed. Then she would leave early in the morning, before they arose and began their day.

During those days, India would panhandle outside of a nearby hamburger joint until she got enough money to go inside and get something to eat. She was adamant that the baby, growing within, must not be affected by the turmoil without. She would also spend a lot of time in the park, weary of wandering. It at least had public facilities, something which she had taken for granted until now.

India would often visit her beloved grandmother's gravesite at the cemetery which was across the street from the park, gathering flowers to place at her grave. She would kneel on her grandmother's grave, and pray, asking God for strength, and imploring Him to guide her and guard her, and to take her by the hand, and lead her in the way in which she should go. On the grounds of the cemetery, was a lovely little bathroom where India would go and refresh herself. It had a vanity seat, but no mirror, and she wondered if, perhaps there was some sort of superstition connected with having a mirror in a cemetery. Yet, she could wash up, and wash out her undergarments, sitting there at the vanity until they dried enough to put back on. It was so peaceful, and no one ever disturbed her there. She would think about her grandma and all the cherished memories they had shared. She thought about how her grandmother had told her, shortly before her death, that she had dreamed that India had a beautiful baby girl. "Talk about a pretty baby!" she'd exclaimed.

The little bathroom, amidst a host of gravesites, was the only place where India felt a sense of serenity. It became her special place. Her grandmother had passed away ten years prior, and India missed her terribly. She had been her grandmother's pride and joy, her shining star, and the apple of her eye ever since the day she was born. And no one else had ever loved India more, certainly not her mother. When she was hospitalized on her deathbed, her grandmother's roommate had told India that she called out her name in her sleep every night. Then Grandma had tearfully confessed to India that she was unafraid of dying, but that she was terrified at the thought of having to leave her alone. Even then, things were bad between India and her mother. But since her grandma's death, things had gone from bad to worse.

India had actually been jailed on three different occasions in the past for attempting to speak with her mother, after she'd gotten the restraining order.

India had only two friends who'd stuck by her. They were the parents of a girl whom she'd grown up with, and they lived directly across the street from her mother. She referred to them as "Momma" and "Pop" because Pop had informally adopted her upon her own father's demise, when she was seven years old. And she had grown to establish a closer relationship with Momma than she'd ever had with her own mother. During this time, India spent a lot of time with them, but they drew the line at taking her in because they feared repercussions from her mother, whom they had been close friends with for over twenty-five years. But they often fed India and generally made her feel at home whenever she was there. She had even given the Social Security office their address, and her check finally arrived there. It was for twice the usual amount because two months had passed.

India still had not tried to contact Bernard. She was sure that he had gone to the apartment, only to find that she was no longer there. And he had no idea where she was or what had befallen her.

After cashing her check, India got a motel room, and, while taking a long leisurely bath, she decided that her best course of action was to get away. She thought that she could out distance all the pain and torment that was plaguing her. She would go to Georgia, her birthplace. She had been there in recent years to visit relatives, and the woodsy, down-home atmosphere proved so peaceful in stark contrast to concrete, crime ridden streets of Southern California. So, the following day, she was on a bus destined for Columbus, Georgia.

But she refused to leave before buying a Money Order in the amount of her rent, and dropping it in the mail slot at the realty office. In hindsight, when she was on the bus, staring out the window, she thought that that had to be the stupidest things she'd ever done. Yet, it had been the foremost thing on her mind ever since she had been evicted, so paying her rent was almost an unconscious act.

During the three day trip, she concentrated on her unborn baby, which was now stirring inside her. She closed her eyes, and placing her hand on her belly, she thought that everything was going to be alright. After all that had occurred, and the loss of everything which had been taken from her, she had her child safely within her, and that was the most precious gift of all.

It was hard to sleep on the bus, so India would gaze out the window at the reflected countryside, and sing softly to herself whispering psalms and hymns that she had learned from her beloved grandmother. She also prayed fervently within her spirit that her baby would be born strong and healthy and that she would be settled, safe and secure, by her birth. She hoped that Bernard was right, in that she was having a girl. She dreamed of adorning her in lovely little pastel dresses, and spoiling her rotten while watching her grow and flourish, nourished with all the love that India already possessed for her.

She would marvel at the spectacular sunrises and sunsets and finally after three days, she arrived in Columbus.

Chapter Four

I will lift up mine eyes unto the hills, from whence cometh my help.
Psalms 121:1

India's sojourn across the country proved not to be the end of her sorrows, as she had hoped, but rather the nightmare continued. Apparently, Momma and Pop had told India's mother about her plans and she, in turn, had immediately contacted her Aunt Hattie, who, before, had welcomed her with open arms, hugging her so tight that she'd actually lifted her off of the floor. But now, India's mother had poisoned Hattie's mind against her, telling her that if India came there not to let her in, and instructing her to call the police.

Totally unaware, India took a cab from the bus station to Hattie's house, and was met with hostile anger instead of the warm, southern hospitality that she was expecting, and was accustomed to being greeted with. Hattie didn't call the police, but she did tell India that she was not welcome in her house, and she refused to listen to reason. All she would say was that she had spoken with India's mother. But India wondered what on earth her mother could have told Hattie that would turn her against her in her hour of need.

The only thing left to do was to go to the Rescue Mission which served the Columbus area. India was exhausted from the long bus trip, and she longed for someplace, any place, to rest her weary head.

The kindness of strangers is what she encountered at the Mission. And that, along with a warm, clean bed was just what she needed.

India used this time at the Mission to reaffirm and strengthen her waning faith. She read her Bible, which she carried everywhere with her, and found reassurance, especially in the Psalms. And she would attend the small church on the Mission grounds, and sing her heart out, while worshipping God with prayer and thanksgiving. After the services, several people would come up to her and compliment her on her beautiful voice.

There were also counselors at the Mission who spoke encouragingly to the lost and brokenhearted souls there and tried to give them direction. India's counselor had asked her if there was someone whom she could call on for help. If so, they could send her there. The only person India could think of was Father Waywood, a Catholic priest. He has befriended her and helped her on her way after her car had broken down once in Pecos, Texas while she was driving from California to Georgia a few years ago. She was sure that Father Waywood was her beacon of hope. When India relayed the story to her counselor, she said that she would work on getting India a bus ticket to Pecos, Texas and would let her know within a few days.

The following day India was deep in her scripture reading when the counselor came with the good news that they would, indeed, be able to buy her a ticket to Texas. India thanked her profusely and sighed a sigh of relief. She looked down at her Bible, and reread the passage she'd been reading when the counselor entered: *"When my father and my mother forsake me, then the Lord will take me up."*

No matter what had gone wrong, or why, she still counted her blessings, feeling so abundantly blessed because of the baby stirring inside her. India was now nearly seven months pregnant. She didn't have much time left to establish a home and some kind of stability for herself and her child. She left Georgia on a Friday night, and arrived in Texas the following evening. She went directly to St. Catherine's Church, and inquired about Father Waywood.

A saintly, old gentleman greeted her. "Hello. I'm Father Barringer. Father Waywood is no longer here. He presides over a parish in El Paso now," Father Barringer explained. India was visibly shaken as she introduced herself.

"Hello Father. My name is India."

"How may I be of assistance?" Father Barringer asked.

"I must speak with Father Waywood," India insisted.

"Why don't we call him?" Father Barringer suggested, and led India to his office inside of the rectory. When he got Father Waywood on the phone, he told him that there was someone who wished to speak with him, and handed India the telephone.

"Father Waywood, this is India Crown. Do you remember helping me a few years ago, after I got stranded on my way to Georgia?" India asked timidly.

"Of course I remember you, dear," Father Waywood announced.

India breathed a sigh of relief and began to relay her predicament, but she broke into a flood of tears as she attempted to convey to him how she was pregnant, homeless and alone. Father Waywood instructed her to put Father Barringer back on the phone. They spoke briefly, and, after they had said their goodbyes, Father Barringer told India that he was going to put her up in a nearby motel. She dried her tears, and managed to thank him through her sobs.

He helped her into his car and made friendly conversation as they drove, first to a convenience store, where he bought a variety of different snacks for her. India asked him if she might have some ice cream, and he smiled and added it to the other goodies. He paid for the items, and they were on their way. At the motel, India waited in the car while Father Barringer got her a room, then carried her bag and groceries in and made sure that she would be comfortable, before leaving.

That night, when saying her prayers, India thanked God for Father Waywood and Father Barringer, and all of the other saints who dedicated their lives to the service of God, so selflessly. Once again, tears streamed down her cheeks, but now, they were tears of joy. She closed her eyes and turned up the covers on the warm, crisp bed. Tomorrow was Sunday. She would go to mass at St. Catherine's and ask God to continue to guard and guide her. She must still, somehow, prepare a nest for her young, and her time, her finest hour, was growing nearer and nearer.

India arose early the next morning, giving herself enough time to walk to the church. On the way, a song popped into her head, and she began to sing softly, to herself. *"When you're weary, feeling small, and friends just can't be found, like a bridge over troubled water, I will lay me down . . ."*

As she was thinking that Father Barringer was her bridge over troubled waters, a car pulled up alongside her, and a young man asked her if she needed a ride. India told him that she was on her way to St. Catherine's Church for mass, and he told her to hop in, as he reached over and opened the door for her.

When they pulled up to the church and stopped, India invited the young man to join her for mass. He smiled politely, but declined, so India exited the car, and thanked him for the lift.

Mass had not yet started and people were just settling into the pews. India knelt down and prayed silently. She thanked God for the child within her which was such a blessing, and which she had grown to love immensely and immeasurably as yet unseen. She counted all her blessings, and prayed that the evil which had befallen her would soon diminish and disappear.

India sat silent and still throughout the mass, her eyes riveted on Father Barringer, as she clung to his every word. She received communion, along with the rest of the congregation. And then, after the mass had ended and Father Barringer had shook holy hands and bid farewell to the procession of parishioners at the door, he asked India to meet him at the altar. Then he sprinkled her with holy water, whispering a special and sacred blessing for her and her child. He then asked her to come to his office. Father Barringer sat behind his desk, his hands clasped as if in prayer. He hesitated for a moment before speaking. "I feel that you should return to California," he explained. "I'd be more than willing to purchase you a bus ticket if there is anyone there in whose care I could place you." India thought of Momma and Pop, and gave him their telephone number. He immediately called them and asked if they would be willing to care for her if she returned to California. When they agreed that they would, he arranged for them to meet her at the bus station in Pasadena, upon her arrival. Then he drove her back to her room at the motel, and admonished her to get a good night's sleep, as he would send someone to take her to the bus station in the morning.

But India didn't sleep well at all that night. She lay in bed and watched the car lights from the highway race across the ceiling and the walls of her room until the wee hours of the night. When they began to hypnotize her, she finally drifted off to sleep. But her sleep was far from restful. In fact, it was fitful because she was full of doubts and despair about her future. She wondered what would become of her and the baby she had yearned for for so long. She just hoped and prayed that Momma and Pop had been sincere in their promise to help her. She couldn't help but wonder why they would have a change of heart after they had made it quite clear to her that they could not take her in. She wondered why all of her so-called friends had abandoned her in her hour of need. She had grown up with Dora, Momma and Pop's daughter, and they had always said they were sisters. Yet, she had brazenly laughed out loud at India once when she was trying to sleep in her car.

Then there was Carrie. They had gone all through high school together as the best of friends. But, just recently on night, India had wandered over Carrie's house and asked her if she might find solace for the night on her bedroom floor. But Carrie had denied her shelter, sending her back out into the cold dark of night.

India wondered what she was returning to. She finally decided that things just had to get better because they certainly couldn't get any worse.

The following morning, India awoke later than she'd planned to. She nervously readied herself, gathering her few belongings, and sat on the edge of the bed, trying to compose herself. It wasn't long before there was a knock at the door. She opened it, and smiled broadly at Father Barringer's assistant. He smiled back at her and asked if she were ready to go. She closed the door behind her, and he helped her into the car.

At the bus station he handed her a one-way ticket to California and a twenty dollar bill. She asked him to thank Father Barringer for everything, and then climbed aboard her bus, bound for Los Angeles. As India settled into her seat, she thought, that this must be how a salmon feels as it instinctively swims upstream, braving the currents, to spawn its young. And it had indeed been an uphill battle, but now she was home free. Or, so she thought.

When India arrived in Los Angeles, she decided that she would call Momma and Pop to let them know when her bus would arrive in Pasadena, so that they could pick her up. She placed a collect call, and when Pop answered the phone the operator asked if he would accept a collect call from India. He answered, "No," and hung up the phone. With his response still echoing in her ears, India hung up the receiver as she tried to fight back the tears. She felt an overwhelming sense of betrayal and bewilderment. She was struggling to find her way, but she felt that she was merely going in circles. Not knowing what else to do, she boarded the bus for Pasadena as scheduled. But once there, she had to come to terms with the sinking realization that there was no one to call, and no place to go.

Counting her change, she found that she had just enough to catch the city bus to Momma's and Pop's house. So she grabbed her bag, which contained everything she owned, and made her way to the bus stop. When she got off the bus, she walked slowly to the house, not knowing what to expect. Once there, Momma and Pop were friendly enough, as always, but explained that she could not stay there. They gave her no reason, but India suspected that, although deep in their hearts they wanted to let her stay, they feared repercussions from their daughter, Dora, who seemed so amused at India's sufferings. And also from India's own mother, who seemed to have a personal vendetta against her. She refused to help her, and prevented anyone who would, even now, in her delicate condition.

Once, a few months back, India had gotten a cab over to a good friend of her mother's to seek help from her. She was a retired beautician who had done India's hair since she was about three years old. India had hoped that she would be willing to take her in, if only for the night. But when she'd arrived there, Rose had called India's mother, who instructed her to call the police. She had tried to poison her mind against her, just as she had Hattie's, in Georgia.

And now, at Momma's and Pop's house, India refused to beg them to let her stay. Once of the few things she still possessed was her pride. So she simply bid them farewell and left.

She had grown up in this neighborhood, on this street, but now, everything was foreign to her. She could return to the old, parked car in the neighbor's driveway up the street, but she had a restless spirit. And so, she decided to walk. She walked and walked and walked, as she wondered why Momma and Pop had lied to Father Barringer. She hadn't asked them and decided that there could be no reason which she would ever understand.

It was getting late, but India still walked, as if in a daze. She had hidden her bag in Momma's and Pop's garage to lighten her load, but he burden was not lifted. She couldn't remember when she had ever been so afraid, and so all alone. India stopped and hesitated at a pay phone. Suddenly, she picked up the receiver and dialed 911.

"What is your emergency?" asked a female voice at the other end. India tried to speak but couldn't.

"Hello? What is your emergency?" the voice inquired again, this time with a sense of urgency.

"I need help . . ." India managed to confer and then she burst into tears.

The 911 dispatched confirmed India's location and India glanced around at nearby street signs, and was able to verify it. The dispatcher told India to stay there, and an officer would arrive in a few minutes. India hung up the phone, and sat down on the curb, crying uncontrollably, her head in her hands. She didn't know how much time had passed when a police car pulled up alongside the curb, and two police officers exited.

They proceeded to question India was obvious concern. "What is your name? Where do you live, and why are you out alone so late at night?" they quizzed. But, but that time, she was hysterical. So much so that she was almost unaware of them helping her up from the curb, and gingerly placing her in the back seat of the patrol car.

After talking briefly among themselves, they attempted to console India. "Things can't be that bad . . . you're going to be just fine," they assured her. When they started up the car, India had no idea where they could be taking her. But she knew that she had not committed any crime, so she could not be going to jail. Her guess was that they were probably transporting her to a mental hospital for evaluation. And she was right.

Chapter Five

Will the unicorn be willing to serve thee, or abide by thy crib?
Job 39:9

India didn't remember much of being admitted to the hospital that night. She woke up the next morning in a dormitory style room with seven other women, varying in age and degrees of insanity. This was not her first time being at the County Hospital.

Slowly, she rolled out of bed and went to inquire about taking a shower. There was a cart in the day room full of soap and other toiletries. When India reached for a bar of soap, she accidently knocked over several bottles of shampoo, and they fell to the floor.

"Pick it up!" someone screamed at her. When she turned around to see where the deafening demand had come from, she encountered a short Black psychiatric aide with a fierce, almost frightening expression on her face.

"Pick it up!" she repeated.

India was taken aback and decided not to comply with the woman's bitter demand. "No." she answered softly. Before she knew what was happening, the aide had taken her and strapped her into a chair, restraining her hands and feet.

This was just the beginning of a month of abuse and even persecution which India, who was now seven months pregnant, suffered at the hands of staff who misused their position of authority beyond belief. Denying her, and other patients of their human rights to dignity and humane treatment of their illnesses. This perpetuated an atmosphere of perpetual chaos.

The worst of these violations occurred when a severely psychotic woman punched India in the abdomen. Instead of striking her back, India grabbed her wrist and held it tight until the staff rushed over to strap the woman down and gave her a shot. India tried not to panic. She immediately felt some pain, but recalled something she had read about how, if a pregnant woman has a fall or some other type of trauma, the baby is protected by the amniotic fluid, which is a shock absorber of sorts. But, when she went to use the bathroom a little while later, she noticed that she had some spotting.

India washed out her panties and asked to use the telephone to call her doctor. They complied, but had someone in the room with her while she made the call. She left a message on the doctor's service explaining where she was and that she had experienced some spotting, but it seemed to have ceased. Then she went and sat down in the day room and stared at the woman who had hit her, wondering how anyone, crazy or not, could want to harm an unborn baby.

Her thoughts were soon interrupted when Ms. Delatore instructed India to accompany her into an examination room so that she could check her out. Apparently the aide who was in the room when she'd made the call to her doctor had just informed Ms. Delatore that India had experienced some spotting.

"That was a confidential call," India retorted in dismay.

Ms. Delatore seemed to be in charge of the unit, but she was not a doctor, so India refused the examination. Ms. Delatore then told India that she had two choices. She could let her examine her, or she could have for men "help her" to restrain India if she refused. India told Delatore that she didn't know exactly who she thought she was, but she was not a physician, and she would not allow her to play doctor with her.

Delatore then called for her back-up. Soon, she and four men were escorting India to an empty room. India offered no resistance because she didn't want to be manhandled, or risk any further harm to her unborn baby, who had just been traumatized already.

Delatore ordered India to lie down on the bed and remove her pants and panties, and lift up her top. India slowly complied, as the four men glared on. One of them asked Delatore, "Do you want us to take off her bra?" His hopes were dashed when she replied, "No. That's alright."

As India lay there, nude from the waist down, Delatore told her to spread her legs, as she donned a pair of rubber gloves and inserted a cold, steel instrument in India's vagina.

India closed her eyes, trapping the tears, and imagined that, this must be how Jesus felt, nailed to the cross, as his tormenters mocked him, having stripped him of his dignity, thus turning his glory into shame.

"Check her panties," Delatore commanded. One of the four flunkies picked up India's panties from off of the bed, and examined them. When he found no sign of blood, Delatore snatched the instrument from India's body and exclaimed, "You didn't have any spotting!" Then she walked out of the room followed by her companions in crime.

India grabbed a sheet, and covered herself. The flood gates of her eyelids could hold back the tears no longer, and they poured down her cheeks, and into her ears as she sobbed silently from the depths of her sorrowful soul. She felt like she had just been brutally raped. She gasped in astonishment. The bitch couldn't even fathom that India had immediately washed out her panties.

Finally, after what seemed like hours, gripped in horror, India arose and put back on her clothes. She felt defiled, demeaned, and disillusioned. She walked back to the day room and began to scream, "You raped me! You raped me with a foreign object! You raped me . . ."

Delatore looked shocked, and began to tremble. Soon, she was shaking like a leaf. It was as if she had no idea of the travesty which she had committed. The next day, India passed Delatore in the hallway on her way to breakfast. Delatore looked as if she wanted to say something, but didn't know what to say.

"Good morning, Ms. Delaroach," India mocked in a sickeningly sweet voice. Delatore looked shocked, but still said nothing. But later that afternoon, she came to India and gleefully exclaimed, "India, you're going to Camarillo!" This time, India was speechless. She had heard such horrific things about Camarillo State Hospital. Suddenly, all of her anger turned into fear.

She sat silently until they called for her. As she slowly approached the staff, one man stood out. He was holding restraints with which to chain her, like an animal. She stood, staring at him as he tied the restraints around her wrists, her waist, and ankles. She thought she smelled alcohol on his breath.

The ambulance drivers threatened India not to make them have to stop for any reason. They didn't have to say what would happen, and she decided that she didn't want to know.

It was a long ride to Camarillo, but finally, they arrived. After delivering India to the staff there, the drivers removed the chains and disappeared. India asked if she could use the bathroom. One of the nurses showed her to the restroom. As she sat on the toilet, she noticed something shining at her feet. Upon picking it up, she discovered that it was a mangled gold necklace with the symbols of faith, hope, and charity dangling from the twisted and tangled chain. She took it to be a sign of good luck, and hid it in her bra, before exiting the bathroom. The nurse was waiting for her, and she conducted a brief physical, taking India's blood pressure and temperature.

"How many months are you?" inquired the nurse.

"About seven, I think," responded India, who was beginning to feel a little more at ease.

"Well, we'll have the doctor examine you." The nurse informed her.

As they escorted India to the mental ward, she noticed a strange smell within the hallways. She thought it smelled like death. This was certainly no place for her, so full of life.

As India gazed around at the patients, she noticed one familiar face, it was that of a Black woman whom she'd met years ago in another hospital, after her illness had first manifested itself, unexpectantly rearing its ugly head, like a monster, which had transformed her entire life from that point on.

The woman spotted India, and recognizing her, she immediately approached her and began to touch her tenderly, caressing her abdomen and stroking her arms. For some reason, India didn't mind.

She smiled at the woman and said, "Hello, I remember you from Metropolitan, but I've forgotten your name."

"Freda" the woman spoke in a whisper. "I remember you."

From that moment, Freda became India's handmaid, pawning over her and succumbing to her every whim. She gave India long intense backrubs, and she would brush her hair, which relaxed her above measure, even transcending her, so that she imagined that she was someplace else, far from the madness which surrounded her.

After a few days, India was taken to get a physical. The doctor examined her and then he, literally, pushed the baby farther into her womb. India had been feeling pressure on her uterus when she walked, and this ceased after the doctor's procedure.

All in all, Camarillo wasn't half as bad as she had imagined. They even brought a cake to the unit when India's birthday rolled around. Freda gave India her cake and continued to lavish her with attention.

India reluctantly decided to call her mother on her birthday. She hadn't spoken to her in months. She called collect and was surprised when her mother accepted the call. India explained how she had been to court, but the judge refused to release her from the hospital because she no place to go. She asked her mother to send some money so that she could catch the bus back to Pasadena. She was crushed when her mother adamantly refused saying, "At least you have a roof over your head."

Chapter Six

They shall not labor in vain, nor bring forth for trouble;
for they are the seed of the blessed of the Lord,
and their offspring with them.
Isaiah 65:23

India continued to endure unspeakable trials and tribulation until, at last, the time of her delivery approached. Luckily, the baby was born two full months overdue, or else it would have been born at Camarillo State Hospital.

After what seemed like an eternity, India had finally been rescued from the institution by two social workers who somehow learned of her dismal dilemma. They placed her in a Board and Care Home in Los Angeles, owned by a young Black woman with two daughters. India had befriended the girls, and they confided in her that their mother planned to take the baby as soon as it was born. So, once again, India had left, gathering all of her clothes and the things she had bought for the baby. She made it to a pay phone and called Momma and Pop. This time, they came through. India had never been happier to see anybody when they reached the location she'd given them on the phone. They grabbed the bags from her arms and drove her back to their house. But by now, she knew better than to stay, so she left. She called her mother and told her that the baby's birth was imminent and she had no one else to turn to, and no place to go.

"Go to the depot," was her mother's suggestion. The Depot was a homeless shelter frequented by derelicts, alcoholics, and drug addicts. The words seemed to burn in India's ears as she hung up the phone.

India refused to accept the fact that her mother gave less than a damn about her and her own grandchild. So, the following day, she walked to the private college where her mother was a professor. Exhausted and weak from the long walk, she went to her mother's office and asked to see her.

"Whom shall I say is calling?" asked the secretary at the front desk.

"Her daughter," gasped India.

When her mother emerged from her office with the look of scorn and disgust apparent on her face, she gestured to India to follow her down the hall.

"What do you want?" she scolded.

"I'm hungry," India spoke softly. "Can you give me some money to get something to eat?"

Her mother went in her purse and handed India seven dollars.

"Here, take this. But if you ever come here again, I'll have you arrested!" she scowled.

"I might want to attend this college," India countered.

"You'd have to get by me," her mother struck back before storming away.

India was aghast. Her spirit was broken. She had always heard it said that your mother is your best friend. But, in her case, this couldn't be farther from the truth, because her mother had become her worst enemy. No one else had ever caused her more pain. And it was a throbbing pain which pierced through to her very soul, and even diminished her essential essence. India wondered how she could possibly sleep at night, not knowing if her past term, pregnant daughter was dead or alive. How could anyone ever despise their own offspring in such a depraved and deplorable manner.

She recognized that she already possessed an endearing and enduring love for her child, whom she had yet to see. And she knew that she would cherish that unconditional love, and that it could only grow with time. She walked away and went to a nearby cafeteria to nourish her depleted body.

So, India was homeless once again when on September 22, 1989, she went into labor while resting in Momma's and Pop's backyard.

When the first pain caught her off guard, she yelled in the house to Pop, "What time is it?"

"5:15" was his reply.

"I just felt a pain," India informed him. Immediately, he and Momma rushed outside and brought her into the house. India lay down in the den on the couch, as the pains became more intense and more frequent. Momma pulled out her bottle of Seagrams 7 and poured herself a drink. Then another. India vaguely overheard her talking to her sister on the phone.

"What do you do when someone's about to have a baby in your house?" Momma inquired.

There was silence for a second, before Momma said, "India. India is right here about to have a baby."

The pangs became excruciating and India didn't know what to do. She arose from the couch and went and locked herself in the bathroom and sat down on the toilet. Soon she heard Momma's voice exclaim, "Open this door. I have a key to this door." Momma left briefly, and, returned with the key. She opened the bathroom door and found India squatting on the toilet moaning in pain. "You could have this baby in my commode." "Get up," Momma ordered.

India obeyed, and Momma led her to one of the twin beds in the guest room and turned down the covers. India crawled in and continued to travail as the labor pains grew closer together. She didn't know where Pop had disappeared to.

India was wondering if, perhaps, Momma was planning to deliver the baby herself, when she heard the kitchen door slam. It was Dora. "Call an ambulance," she demanded. "India could die or the baby could die," she screeched.

Then Dora and Momma left, and the next thing that India heard was Pop on the phone, calling for an ambulance.

When she arrived at Huntington Memorial Hospital, the same hospital where India's beloved Grandmother had died, Dora and Momma arrived soon thereafter. India was relieved to see Momma, who stood watch over her as she lie on the gurney panting frantically to subdue the intense pain.

India yelled to the nurse to bring her a bed pan because she had to have a bowel movement. The nurse appeared and explained that it was probably the baby, bearing down on her cervix. India had lost all track of time. All that she was aware of was the pain, which seemed to strike like lightning bolts. Finally, an attendant came and wheeled India to the delivery room. The nurse asked her if she wanted her companions in the room with her. India told her to tell them to come back in the morning. She was left alone, except for the intermittent visits by the burse to check how far she had dilated. Finally, the nurse informed the young doctor on call that India was fully dilated. And it wasn't long before the doctor exclaimed, "It's a girl. She's perfect!"

The nurse whisked the baby to the opposite end of the room, and the next thing India heard was her newborn wailing. By this time, the doctor had begun to stitch her up, and India also began to wail.

"I want to see my baby," she cried.

The nurse brought the baby over, and placed her in India's waiting arms. "Look at her eyelashes," exclaimed the nurse, smiling broadly at the beautiful child. India looked at her baby's closed eyes. Her long eyelashes lay almost on her cheeks. After all, she was a full two months overdue, and had perfected all of her features.

India lay on her side, with her newborn baby girl cradled in the crux of her arm, shielding her like a mother eagle. The baby stopped crying. India thought she looked like an angel. She had planned to name her Ashana, but, now, looking at her, dearly beloved and longed for, she was definitely an Angel, sent from God.

Soon the nurse reappeared to take the baby to the nursery. India kissed her daughter on her tiny forehead before reluctantly relinquishing her.

She woke up in the recovery room with curtains drawn around her. She could see the legs and feet of a new father, standing beside the gurney in the cubicle adjacent to hers. India wondered about Bernard. It had not even occurred to her to call him when she went into labor. And she had not even given him a thought during her nine hours of travail. But now, suddenly, she wanted him there. She longed for him to see the beautiful child which they had created through the magic of their love.

India had not seen Bernard in over a month, when their paths had crossed at the liquor store around the corner from his parent's house. India had been inside the store willing away the time, eating ice cubes from a Styrofoam cup, and staring aimlessly out the window, when Bernard passed by. She had thumped on the window to get his attention, and, when he saw her, so great with his child, he turned around and entered the store. But he'd walked right past her, as though frightened by her fragile condition. They had not seen each other since the night that he'd spilled his guts before India had been evicted.

After a few minutes, he'd turned around, but he had disappeared to the back of the store, where the owners, who were friends of his, resided. India had exited the store without so much as speaking a word to Bernard. And she had no inkling when she would see him again.

When they brought the baby to India's room, early the next morning, India realized the breadth of the baby's beauty. Her full head of hair was combed, parted on the side, and it framed her perfect pink face . . . Bernard's face. The baby was the spitting image of Bernard. India laughed out loud with joy unspeakable. She fed her precious baby girl, and then laid her upon her breast, above her full heart.

For a moment, India forgot all about her dire circumstances. The fact of the matter was that she was still homeless, and had no place to take her newborn baby girl. So, after the nurse came and took Angel back to the nursery, India made some calls. First, she called Bernard's parent's house. When no one picked up, she left a message.

"I had a girl! She looks just like you. She's gorgeous. We're at the Huntington Hospital." Then she called her mother and left a similar message on her machine when there was no answer. Then she called Momma and Pop. Pop answered the phone.

"I had a girl," India informed him.

" . . . a girl!" Pop echoed. "We'll be right there."

It wasn't long before Momma showed up. But, instead of Pop, Dora was with her. Momma entered the room first, smiling broadly. "That's the prettiest baby I've ever seen," she exclaimed, after having examined the baby in the nursery. The remark surprised India because Momma had three granddaughters, including Dora's daughter. India returned her smile and recounted her labor and natural childbirth. They all laughed when she got to the part where the baby was crying, and India was crying, while the doctor stitched her up.

They didn't stay long. And, after they left, India called the nurse and asked to speak to the hospital social worker about her circumstances. When the young man entered the room and introduced himself as the social worker, India told him that she was homeless, and had no place to take her baby. She asked him if she could arrange for them to go to some sort of shelter.

The social worker excused himself momentarily, and returned with a young Black woman with a stern countenance. He introduced her, and informed India that she was from the Department of Family and Children's Services. He added that she just happened to be on the premises.

India was immediately suspicious. Why would a social worker from the Department of Family and Children's Services just happen to be there? India decided to give her the benefit of the doubt, and related the state of her affairs to the woman, whose fierce expression never changed. When India had finished speaking, without blinking, the woman asked to speak with the hospital social worker in private. They then retreated to the threshold of the doorway when India looked on. The woman seemed to be doing all the talking while the man nodded.

They returned to India's bedside and the woman blurted out, "We've decided to take the baby." India was stunned. She was both enraged and outraged all at once. But she would not allow herself to plead for her own child, so she said nothing. After an awkward moment of silence, the woman turned and walked away, with the man following behind her. India was in a state of disbelief. How could this be happening? How could everything have gone so terribly wrong? She tried to think positive. The baby was strong, healthy, and beautiful. And India knew that she had to place her in the hands of God. She thought of the Serenity Prayer: *God grant me the serenity to accept the things I cannot change; courage to change the things I can; and the wisdom to know the difference.*

An inexplicable sense of calm came over her; and she was soon asleep for the first time since giving birth. The following morning, India waited for them to bring her baby to her to nurse. When they failed to do so, she arose, and walked to the nursery. There lay her newborn daughter. She was undoubtedly the most beautiful baby in the nursery. No, the most beautiful baby in the world. To India's horror, Angel had a handwritten sign on her tiny chest which read "HOLD." This signified that the baby was not to be brought to her mother. They were treating her helpless child, her only child, which she had so longer for, as if it were an item of clothing on lay-away, which India could not afford to purchase. She was astonished at the cold and callous manner of the hospital staff. Depriving an innocent baby of its mother's warmth and love, of everything with which she was familiar. Her mother's voice, her mother's heartbeat, her mother's unyielding love. It went against every law of nature. India possessed an innate need to nurture and nourish her newborn, and she was abruptly stopped from doing so by one word on a piece of paper.

She returned to her room and crawled underneath the sheet and wept silently, bitterly. But she was sure that God heard her, along with all of his angels. She was unaware of how much time had passed when someone pulled the sheet from off her head. It was Momma. She and Pop had come to pick her up from the hospital. The social worker had given no thoughts as to where India would go from the hospital. Had Momma and Pop not come to her rescue, they would have just released her onto the street, after just having given birth two days prior.

India was vaguely aware of being taken in a wheelchair to Momma's and Pop's awaiting Cadillac. She climbed in the back seat, her destination and destiny unknown.

Chapter Seven

Thus saith the Lord; A voice was heard in Ramah,
lamentation, and bitter weeping; Rachel was weeping for
her children refused
to be comforted for her children, because they were not.
Jeremiah 31:15

After all the blood, sweat, and tears of childbirth, India left the hospital an empty vessel. Momma and Pop delivered her to their sister-in-law's house a few towns away. Her name was Brenda and she was a widow, rearing her ten year old twin grandsons. Momma and Pop stayed only a few minutes before Momma handed India eleven dollars, and they were gone.

Brenda entreated India with disdain for some unknown reason. She immediately had India doing housework, polishing her furniture, and washing walls. And, at mealtimes, she wanted India to eat in the enjoining garage. India refused, and told Brenda that she would not eat at all if she had to eat in the garage. Brenda relented, and allowed India to eat at the dining room table with the boys. Brenda, who was in menopause, seemed to envy the fact that India had just become a new mother, and told her that she wanted the baby, whom she hadn't even seen. But, the clincher was when Brenda referred to India's baby as "a bastard." She had quite some nerve because her grandsons were also illegitimate. Something clicked in India when she heard that cruel remark and she started for the door, not knowing where she was going. She was miles away from Momma's and Pop's house, but she knew she could not withstand hearing her beautiful Angel referred to as a bastard.

Brenda stopped her at the door, and apologized profusely. "I'm so sorry. Please forgive me," Brenda pleaded. "I wish I had a baby."

"My coming here was a bad idea, it's not going to work," India uttered.

"If you must leave, at least wait until morning," Brenda implored. India agreed. Besides, she was exhausted, both mentally and physically spent. But, when India arose from her tearstained pillow the following morning, she had not slept a wink. She took a shower and dressed. To her surprise, Brenda called a shuttle bus to transport her to the Greyhound Bus Station and handed her a twenty dollar bill as she walked out the door to board the awaiting schedule.

When India arrived at the Greyhound Station, she bought a ticket to Pasadena which cost a mere fifteen dollars one way. Before long, she was back in Pasadena and instinctively went to Momma's and Pop's house. They looked surprised to see her.

"India, how in the hell did you get here?" Pop inquired.

"I took the Greyhound bus because Brenda was impossible," India responded.

"Lord, have mercy," added Momma.

India did not want to go back to her homeless routine of wandering aimlessly around during the day, and then seeking shelter for the night. So she asked Momma and Pop to take her to the Board and Care Home where she resided before her pregnancy. They conceded. It just so happened that the owner was there when they arrived. He told India that they didn't have any vacancies at that facility, but he did have a place for her at another manor, not far away.

Momma and Pop took India and her meager belongings to her new home. The administrator of the Board and Care Home had been notified of India's arrival by the owner. She showed India to her room upstairs. India was happy to have a room to herself, and began to relax a bit. India climbed into the warm bed, and, for the first time in days, got a good night's sleep.

Although India was comfortable enough at the Board and Care Home, called Hill House, her spirit within her was restless. Her thoughts never strayed far from thinking about Angel, and hoping and praying that she was okay, and that she was being well cared for by her foster parents. She was such a beautiful baby, how could anyone help but to adore her?

After India had been at Hill House for six weeks, her intense longing to see her Angel was fulfilled when the social worker from the Department of Family and Children Services informed her that he was going to take her to visit her baby girl.

After six long, tortuous weeks, India was finally going to see her child, which had been snatched from her breast like a lovely flower, plucked up by its roots. On the morning of the visit, India arose early, showered, and put on her prettiest dress. She only had a few clothes because she had suffered the loss of all of her precious belongings after having moved around so much.

When the social worker arrived to pick her up, she was waiting outside. The night before, she had phoned her mother to tell her that she was going to visit Angel, and to ask her if she had a camera, that she could borrow to record the special occasion. Her mother had snapped that she didn't have a camera, and hung up the phone.

Now, as India tried to erase the sharp rejection from her mind, she walked quickly to the awaiting car and got in. The social worker introduced himself as "Paul," and India told him it was nice to finally meet him in person. They had spoken over the telephone, and he had assured India that Angel was in good hands. But she needed to see for herself. She had tried to deal with the overwhelming emptiness she felt since Angel had been taken away. But she could not rest assured until she saw that Angel was okay, and held her in her longing arms.

When they drove up to the foster home, India was surprised to see a "For Sale" sign in the yard, but she said nothing. Angel's foster mother let them in and Paul introduced India to her. India was surprised again to see that she was Mexican. She seemed cold. India spotted a bassinette in the living room and immediately and instinctively drew near it.

"Is this my angel?" she asked.

"Yes," the woman answered.

India's heart melted as she gathered the baby in her arms, and sat down on the couch. Paul and the woman sat across from her.

The baby began to cry, and India fought back her own tears when she noticed that Angel had broken out in a rash on her face and arms. "Tell mommy all about it," India cooed in baby talk.

"Say Mommy, who are these people?" She began to rock back and forth as she held the baby close. Angel stopped crying and India loosened her grip to look into her lovely eyes. She was even more beautiful than

India remembered. And in her six weeks of life, she had grown to look even more like Bernard. Her thick, black hair covered her head, and the back of her neck. And she looked almost like she belonged in the family of Hispanics.

India began to undress Angel and adorn her with the outfit she had bought for her. An exquisite pink dress with a matching bonnet. When she took off her undershirt, she noticed that the rash was all over Angel's upper torso. "Why does she have this rash?" India demanded.

"She's going to the doctor tomorrow," the woman countered nonchalantly. India asked her if she had any Vaseline and the woman handed her a jar of the ointment. India began to anoint the baby's patches of scales. She was sure that it had been caused by her nerves, from being deprived and uprooted from the only thing that had been familiar to her, her mother's warmth and love. Whoever heard of a six week old infant with a nervous condition? India asked the woman for a bottle, and Angel absorbed the formula as if she were starving. India burped the baby before cradling her in her arms. She felt fulfilled, and didn't know how she could ever leave her again. She began to sing softly to the baby. *Mama's little baby loves shortening, shortening, Mama's little baby loves shortening bread . . .* It was a song that was near and dear to her, sung to her throughout her childhood by her beloved grandmother. *Put on the skillet, put on the lead, Mamma's gon cook a little shortening bread.* Soon the baby was sound asleep in India's arms. She looked like a doll, dressed in the adorable pink dress and bonnet. India turned to Paul, "Maybe we should go while she's asleep."

Paul nodded and smiled.

India arose and returned the baby to her bassinette, placing a holy kiss upon her cheek.

A wave of sadness flooded over India as she, once again, had to leave her baby girl. She remained silent on the way back until, when they were almost at Hill House, India spoke up and asked Paul to drop her off at the cemetery where her Grandma was buried. The day marked the eleventh anniversary of her passing, and India needed to acknowledge it.

She stood over the grave and read the inscription aloud, *Beloved mother and grandmother . . . she gave so much, and asked so little.* India began to sing, softly. *Momma's little baby loves shortening, shortening. Momma's little baby loves shortening bread . . .* Then she turned and began the long walk back to Hill House, humming the sacred lyrics as she strode.

By the time she arrived back, India had decided that she must leave California in order to be able to secure a home for her Angel. The rent in California was sky high and there was simply no way she could afford an apartment there. She decided to return to Georgia. The plan was to get the baby back once she established a home for her. The only thing holding her here was Angel, but she wasn't doing her any good by being one step away from homeless.

India gave notice that same day that she would be leaving the manor. She would wait for her SSI check to arrive on the first, and then purchase a one-way ticket to Columbus. She had totally lost contact with Bernard, and nothing had changed between her and her mother. So it was up to her to forge a future for Angel and herself. She was certain that this was the right course of action to take. In fact, it was the only viable option she had. She would believe, she could dream, she could will, but ultimately she had to act on her faith, and place her uncertain future in the hands of God.

Chapter Eight

They have healed also the hurt of the daughter of my people slightly,
saying peace, peace; when there is no peace.
Were they ashamed when they had committed abomination?
Nay they were not ashamed neither could thy blush
therefore they shall fall among them that fall:
at the time that I visit them they shall be cast down, Saith the Lord.
Jeremiah 6:14, 15

On December 1st, India departed, once more for Columbus, Georgia. She'd been given her SSI check by the administrator of Hill House, who had dropped her off at the Greyhound Bus Station.

India felt hopeful as the bus pulled off, as opposed to the dire hopelessness she had felt in her past journey. She relaxed, and even became friendly with some of the other passengers on the bus. A few of them teased her about her loud snoring after she'd dozed off in her seat.

By the time the bus arrived in Columbus, India had devised a plan. She had an old acquaintance take her to the mental hospital, where she told the psychiatrist who screened her that she was suicidal after having lost custody of her newborn daughter. She didn't have to try too hard to sound convincing, and was immediately admitted to the hospital.

India had been there before, and she recalled the beautiful, spacious grounds, complete with a lake. Although some of the staff were completely incompetent, misusing and abusing their authority, the facility, overall, was a decent place for her to recuperate from the terrible blow that life had inflicted upon her.

The following day, as India sat in the dining room, enjoying a breakfast of ground beef, country biscuits and gravy, her eyes fixed on a man across the room. He was a White man, about India's age, and something about him stirred up a crazy commotion inside her. She inquired about him to a girl at her table, and found out that his name was Danny. During the next few days, India managed to get acquainted with Danny, and discovered that they were kindred spirits. They both delighted in each other's presence. And Danny confessed that when he'd first seen her, he had remarked to a friend at his table that "That bitch got some legs!"

Danny was there because he actually attempted suicide, slitting his wrists in a Georgia hotel room. He was from Florida, and after driving aimlessly, in a state of despondency, following a terrible breakup with his girlfriend, he had decided that life was not worth living. India gave Danny her Gideon's Bible which she herself had taken from a hotel room, and they gave another new found hope. They would sit together on Bingo night, and take long walks around the lake. India and Danny found in each other exactly what the other needed, namely companionship that blossomed into a true mutual fondness.

India was released from the hospital before Danny, after about three weeks. She succeeded in getting an apartment in Columbus, a small efficiency with one room, a bathroom and a kitchen. The rent was only $150 per month, and it was furnished with a double bed, dresser, table, and an oversized chair and a stove and refrigerator. India went to K-Mart and purchased everything she needed to make it a home. She bought beautiful bedding and towels, a cookware and dinnerware set, and transformed the place into a comfortable shelter from the turbulent storm which had been her life of late.

India kept in contact with Danny through letters and phone calls, and invited him to come and live with her when he was released from the hospital. He wrote her an emotional love letter in which he stated that he could envision the two of them growing old together.

The day that Danny showed up at India's door, a few weeks later, she was ecstatic. He surprised her by falling asleep beside her that night without even touching her. She had been longing to melt in his arms, but, he later informed her that he didn't want her to think he was like all the other guys who had been trying to get in her pants. She had written to him about all the men who had tried to seduce her.

A few days passed before she and Danny made love, and she had to coax him by asking, "Danny, will you suck the milk from my breasts so

I won't have to express myself?" Her request was followed by an intense culmination of what had come to be their evident love.

The following day, India took Danny to the sanctified spot that she had found while exploring the neighborhood, just a few short blocks away. It was on the edge of the Chattahoochee River, which separated Columbus, Georgia from Phenix City, Alabama. They would often retreat there, and sit, silently, in one of the gazebos which lined its beautiful bank. Lost in their own thoughts, they would linger there leisurely, at every opportunity, before strolling back to their harmonious abode, hand in hand.

The days and nights that followed were the stuff that dreams were made of. India enjoyed cooking for Danny, and he was satiated with her substance. They would get drunk and dance outside, in the moonlight and then make passionate love before falling asleep basking in the warmth of each other's arms, where nothing on earth could do them any harm.

Danny found a job within a week. Or rather, the job found him. He was outside, having a beer with one of their neighbors, when the owner of the building, a middle aged White woman showed up. She took one look at Danny and offered him a job with her property management company. India and Danny both knew that the woman was infatuated with him, but the job paid him in cash every Friday. He was an electrician by trade, but now, he did everything from painting, to installing drywall at various properties. The woman was constantly trying to get Danny to work late, but he would simply tell her that India had his dinner waiting, and he had to get home.

During that time, India was in contact with Angel's social worker at the Department of Family and Children's Services, who allowed her to call, collect each week to inquire about Angel. It was through one of these calls that India learned that Angel had been moved to another foster home. Her first foster mother had died suddenly from a brain aneurysm. The foster father was devastated and had tried to keep Angel, as he, and his wife had been planning to adopt her. But, Angel was taken from him and placed in a home in Pasadena.

India tried to imagine how her baby felt in being traumatized yet again, having been taken away from all that was familiar to her, and transplanted, once again in a foreign environment. She couldn't help but feel that what had happened was simply karma. That Almighty

God had required a sacrifice for the unspeakable abomination that had transpired.

India also found out that her mother had been to the new home, which was not far from her, to visit Angel. She decided to call her. To her surprise, her mother accepted the collect call, and actually sounded pleasant. She had been to see her new granddaughter who was now seven months old, and had fallen in love with her. She told India that Angel was in a home with a Black couple and two older foster children, a brother and sister and that she intended to visit her often. By the time India had hung up the phone, she felt that her tortured relationship with her mother was on the mend, and she was glad that Angel was at least her own race.

When India informed Danny of what had occurred, he was heartbroken for "Little Angel," as he called her. "Well, you know what we need to do?" announced Danny. It was more of a declaration than a question.

"What?" answered India, distracted by her unsettling image of Angel amidst strangers, yet again.

"We need to get married and get Little Angel," Danny declared.

The statement took India totally by surprise, and touched her to the core. She tried to remain cool. "You have to propose," she coaxed.

"Marry me," Danny asserted, placing his hand to his heart.

A hush fell over the room before India spoke softly, "Yes, of course I'll marry you."

India was thrilled. The next time she spoke with the social worker, she told her that she and her fiancé wanted to gain custody of Angel. The woman told India that she would initiate an Interstate Pact, whereby India's home would be evaluated by the local Department of Family and Children's Services. Meanwhile, she and Danny began making wedding plans.

The Interstate Pact was set in motion and a social worker was assigned to India. But the victimization continued. When India received the court papers from California, they stated that Angel was placed in foster care because India had abandoned her in the hospital. Also, Angel's father was listed as "a transient" because India had said that she wasn't aware of his whereabouts. She could not comprehend how the system had succeeded in blaming the victim. It was an atrocity. India immediately wrote a rebuttal in the form of a disposition, and mailed it to the court. But she couldn't help but wonder if anyone would even consider her position, if they read it at all.

When India told her mother that she and Danny were planning to wed, she sent them some money, much to India's surprise. She assured her that Angel had adjusted well to her new surroundings, and that June, her new foster mother, cherished her, to the point of doting on her. India felt relieved that her baby daughter was attentively cared for. And life in Georgia was growing more and more blissful.

Every morning, when Danny returned home from a hard day's work, he would envelope India in his arms and give her a long, deep kiss, as if he hadn't seen her in months. He told her that she was the only Black girl he'd ever loved.

On the morning that the social worker, assigned to India's case in the interstate pact, arrived for her initial visit, Danny was at work. India greeted her pleasantly and introduced herself. The woman, in turn, introduced herself as Ms. Baxter. She asked if any of the men who were congregated in the parking lot, drinking beer, was Danny. India told her that Danny was working, and added, "Besides, Danny is White." Ms. Baxter seemed taken aback. "What does he do?" she inquired. "He works for the realty company that owns this building," India answered proudly.

She proceeded to inform Ms. Baxter that she desperately wanted her daughter, and further explained how she intended to move to a larger place to accommodate Angel's need for room to grow. Ms. Baxter seemed unimpressed, to say the least. She kept looking India up and down, and India felt that she might be jealous, as she had an obvious affliction and walked with a limp. India wondered if perhaps she had contracted polio as a child.

When Danny came home, and they were sitting down at dinner, India told him that they were going to have to move if they wanted any chance at all of getting Angel. Danny announced that he couldn't move because the property management had enlisted him to act as the resident manager of their building. India could not hide her disappointment, but, if she was forced to choose between Danny, and even the remote chance of getting Angel back, then, as much as she adored Danny, she would have to choose the latter. She was sure that, if she secured suitable housing, she was certain to get the approval of the court. As she had stated in her written disposition, Angel was her only child, so she had no prior history of child abuse or child neglect.

That night, India and Danny's lovemaking was bittersweet. They both sensed that this could be the beginning of the end.

Chapter Nine

Thou whom I have taken from the ends of the earth,
and called thee from the chief men thereof, and said unto thee,
Thou art my servant; I have chosen thee, and not cast thee away.
Isaiah 41:9

When Angel's first birthday approached, India found herself in a melancholy mood. She realized that she had missed her baby's major milestones. Her first smile, her first tooth, her first steps, her first words. She mailed Angel an adorable white, teddy bear and a T-Shirt that had printed "Somebody in Georgia Loves Me" on the front.

Her mother made sure that Angel got the gift and card, and sent India pictures of Angel in the T-Shirt. She was quite oblivious to the teddy bear, but fascinated by the birthday card, which bore a picture of a baby, smiling broadly, displaying one tooth.

Meanwhile, she had moved into a nice two bedroom, furnished trailer. It was situated in a trailer park that was filled with children playing and riding bicycles, with whom she soon became acquainted. Danny remained at the apartment in virtual servitude to his boss. She even convinced him to shave off his full beard and moustache, telling him he looked like a "mountain man" and needed a more professional appearance. But she had not succeeded in seducing him. India knew this because Danny had begged her to come and spend the night with him and she readily relented. Danny told India how much he missed her, and confided how his boss tried, unsuccessfully to entice him with Harley-Davidsons and frivolous promises of abundant wealth. India listened as she prepare Danny's favorite dinner for him.

"Hell, she had a husband, and a son about my age," he exclaimed.

"Well, I certainly can't blame her for being enthralled by you," India laughed.

After they'd made tender love, Danny embraced India and held her close throughout the night, then awoke caressing her the next morning. He entreated her not to leave until after he went to work.

By the time Ms. Baxter came to inspect India's new home, Danny had quit his job and moved in with her. He chose not to be there when Ms. Baxter arrived because he said he did not want to be scrutinized. India gave Ms. Baxter a tour of the trailer. She showed her the room intended and prepared for Angel which had pictures of her first birthday adorning the walls and a mobile hanging over the twin bed. There was a draft in the room because it was sealed off, as India held it sacred.

Ms. Baxter returned several times before rendering her decision. India was appalled when she ripped open the letter from the Department of Family and Children's Services, which disclosed the fact that she had been denied custody. She could not imagine why, and concluded that the only reason must have been because of her interracial union. She went to the office personally because she wanted Ms. Baxter to look her in the eye and offer one good reason why she found her unfit to rear her only child.

When the receptionist informed India that Ms. Baxter was unavailable, she said she would wait. She waited over two hours until Ms. Baxter was convinced that she was not going to go away. When she finally emerged from her office, she could not even look India in the eye. India demanded to know, in writing, why she had been denied custody of her child. And she had to persist, calling numerous times before she got the letter stating that the decision had been made because India did not have a crib in Angel's room.

Once again, India was infuriated. She knew that could not possibly be the reason, and was merely a flimsy excuse to cover up the blatant prejudice of a jealous, vindictive woman who had been unfavorably biased since learning that India's mate and Angel's perspective step-father was White. It would have been simple enough for India to obtain a crib, had the decision been favorably rendered.

Danny witnessed India's dire devastation, and felt that it was his fault that her child would remain a ward of the court. His guilt was overwhelming and was the core of their subsequent bitter bickering and alienation of each other. When Danny left to visit his parents for Christmas, he did not return from Florida.

India was left alone in her misery. It was around this time that she learned through her mother, that Angel had been placed in a third foster home because her foster father had been accused of molesting the older girl in the home. She said that he had been arrested, and all three children were immediately removed from the home. The only thing greater than India's despair, was that which she imagined that Angel must be experiencing. But she was barely cognitive of that when she grabbed her bottle of psychotropic medication, counted the seventeen pills and swallowed then. Then she retreated to her bed, ceasing to care if she ever awoke to a new dawn.

But God, and all his legions of angels must have been watching over her during the night, because she did awake, the following morning, with someone banging on the door of her trailer. India arose and staggered to the door. She fumbled at the lock before finally opening it. There stood Jerry, a little boy who lived down the road in the trailer park.

"India, Rudy pushed me down off my bicycle," he cried.

India stated to speak, but the words got caught in her throat. She tried again. "Where's your mama" she asked.

"She's gone, are you alright?"

"I'll be okay. Tell Rudy don't make me have to come down there."

"Okay," Jerry consented. He stood there for a moment before India disappeared behind the door. India gazed out her living room window as the little boy turned and got back on his bicycle, and disappeared down the road. He was completely oblivious to the fact that he had probably just saved India's life in preventing her from sleeping the sleep of death.

India continued to stare out the window, as the neat rows of trailers and the still, scenic countryside and whispered a prayer.

"I shall not die, but live, and declare the works of the Lord . . ." she vowed.

That very next day, India decided to return to California. Her master plan had failed, and she needed to be near Angel. She had no earthly idea where she would stay, only that her heart was leading her, and her soul within her fainted to be with her daughter, her reason for living.

Chapter Ten

As one whom his mother comeforteth, so will I comfort you;
And ye shall be comforted in Jerusalem.
Isaiah 66:13

So India sojourned back to California after telling all her friends in Georgia that she would probably not return. Again, she contacted the owner of Board and Care Home where she had resided. This time he placed her in a facility in Los Angeles. The administrator came and picked India up at a motel in Pasadena, where she had checked in upon her arrival. She was a Mexican woman who seemed pleasant enough. She had admonished India about the empty wine bottle on the television in her room. India simply shrugged it off and smiled.

When they arrived at the facility, the woman, named Maria, showed India to her room. It was upstairs, and, again, she was glad that she didn't have a roommate. India settled in, and put her belongings in a chest of drawers. She placed her radio beside the bed. India listened to Classic Rock on the radio constantly, and she was in a state of mind where she believed that every song was a long distance message from Danny to her. Songs like *Cherish, Do you Believe in Magic?* And *Since I Fell For You.* She listened to the radio night and day, and felt that she was communicating with Danny.

After about a week, without any warning, Maria confronted her, saying, "They're coming to get you this evening, whether you like it or not." And sure enough, that evening after dinner an ambulance arrived to transport India to a mental hospital. India was terrified and prayed aloud the entire way of the seemingly endless journey. Her heart was pounding within her as she called to mind some of the cruel persecutions she had suffered at the hands of the inept mental health workers in her past hospitalizations.

But this hospital was quite different. It was in Redondo Beach, and the name of the hospital was South Bay. To India's surprise, it proved to be an almost pleasant experience. The workers were competent and compassionate, and the food was delicious. India remained there for two weeks before she was discharged. And she did not look back.

She left the hospital and found her way to the nearby beach. She strolled along the pier, becoming swallowed up in the sea of people. When night began to befall her, she sat down on a bench, overlooking the ocean, and watched the waves crash against the rocks, along the shore. India noticed the silhouette of a man standing in front of her, leaning against the railing with his back to her. He had a long, black ponytail that reached the middle of his back. The next thing India knew, he was sitting beside her on the bench, talking to her as if they were longtime friends who had just been reunited. His name was J.C. and he was a full-blooded Cherokee India. "I'm homeless," India blurted out, and then waited to see what his response would be. She was totally astounded when he replied, "So am I." His admission just seemed to add to their instant comradeship. "I know where you can sleep," J.C. offered. India hesitated, and was reluctant to go with the handsome stranger. But then she looked deep into his big brown eyes. He had dove's eyes and she arose and went with him to his spot, making light conversation along the way, which somehow seemed familiar.

India felt a deep sense of déjà vu, and felt that she had been destined to meet J.C. He was like an angel, sent from God to protect her from a dubious destiny. God only know what would have befallen her if her anchor had not been there, at that exact time and space, to attend to her necessity.

J.C. and India walked and talked until they came to an apartment building. J.C. stopped and led India behind some tall bushes in front of the building that shielded them from view. There was a space between the building and the bushes that was just big enough for the two of them to lie down comfortably. J.C. told India to stay there while he left momentarily, and reappeared with a blanket. He placed it under them, and they lay down close together, facing each other.

India took J.C.'s head and positioned his mouth to her breast. Instinctively, he began to suck the milk from one, and then the other, as she gently stroked the nape of his neck. Soon, they were both sound asleep. Having granted each other just what the other required.

India and J.C. awoke huddled together like two kittens. She told J.C. that she was going to use the bathroom in the ladies room on the beach. The agreed to meet later on the beach later that morning. India sat on the stair way on the beach which led to some ocean side condominiums. Soon, she felt someone touch her gently on her shoulder. She turned around and smiled at J.C. who was standing over her.

"I have to go baby sit these drunks," he explained.

India soon learned that he had a group of about six or seven homeless friends, and that he had appointed himself their leader, keeping them in line and out of trouble.

So India wiled away the day on the beach. It was so beautiful and serene. She visited the nearby boardwalk with its quaint shops and restaurants, and milled around the businesses, getting lost in the crowd. One kind man even offered to buy her lunch. She readily accepted, and they sat at an outside café and exchanged small talk while eating tostadas.

As the sun began to set majestically over the ocean, India met up with J.C. and his friends in the park. They were all drinking wine, taking turns passing the bottle around. J.C. introduced India to them. "This is my friend," he said, and passed her the almost empty bottle. India took it from him and, turning it all the way up, finished off the potent spirits. This was her communion, as she was initiated into J.C.'s family of travailing travelers. India listened and laughed as they recounted their day. One White guy, Like, with a deep tan and blond hair, turned to India and exclaimed, "What did you do to him? It was this big." He held his hands about a foot apart.

India had no idea what Luke spoke of until after she and J.C. had retreated back to their secret spot. As they lay on the blanket, J.C. took India's hand and placed it to his groin. It felt like he had a snake in his pants. Then J.C. attempted to slip his hand inside India's panties. She grabbed his hand, preventing him. "You're wet," he concluded meaning that she was on her period. It was true. So she and J.C. snuggled together on the blanket as she, once again, nursed him until he fell asleep, comforted and content.

India wondered what would become of her and J.C. They could not continue like this indefinitely. India knew that she had to begin focusing on Angel. After all, that is why she had returned to California in the first place. However, she felt torn because she didn't want to leave J.C. But they were homeless after all, living on a beach.

For over a month, India frolicked with J.C. and his friends. Finally, she faced the fact that it was time to move on and attempt to establish some sense of stability in her life. But there was one thing that she had to do first. She felt that she must seal the bond which she'd formed with J.C., thus manifesting the substance of their primitive love.

One night, as they were all sitting in the park, drinking, before retreating to their respective shelters, India placed her hand on J.C.'s penis. He quickly moved it away, embarrassed.

"J.C., will you go with me to the bathroom?" India asked.

J.C. said nothing but arose and took India's hand, helping her up. He knew exactly what this meant, and it was a moment which he had patiently anticipated. They walked slowly and silently to the public restrooms on the beach. India entered the woman's room, and after checking to make sure no one else was there, she called to J.C.

They went into a stall and locked the door behind them. When India saw the immensity of J.C.'s member, she instructed him to sit on the toilet. Then she turned her back to him, and ever so slowly lowered her body onto his, until she was sitting on his lap with his penis deep inside her.

"Stand up!" he commanded her.

"Sit Down!" "Stand up!" "Sit down!" until J.C. exploded inside of her.

She sat on his lap for a moment while he cupped her breasts in his hands. "Comanche," India gasped, as she arose, slowly. It was a name which she had given him after realizing his mighty splendor and his quiet strength of character.

"Well, what's my mother's name?" challenged J.C.

"Sarah," India had replied.

J.C. was startled.

"That is right," he'd uttered, looking sternly at India in reverent disbelief.

And now, as J.C. and India faced each other, she smiled and said, "You could at least kiss me." He planted a gentle kiss upon her lips. "Open the door," he whispered. "No!" India answered in defiance. "Well, I'll just . . ." and with that J.C. disappeared over the seven foot wall of the bathroom, literally flying upon the wings of the wind.

India stood there, both baffled and in awe of J.C.'s power and might. Finally, she opened the door and exited the bathroom. She found J.C. in the men's room, at the sink, gingerly wiping his penis with toilet tissue. "Are you going to be with me tonight?" she asked, because sometimes he would stay with his friends, carousing the night away.

"No, not tonight," J.C. replied.

"Fuck you, Comanche!" India shouted.

"Comanche," echoed J.C.

India was blown away. She turned and walked to the top of the stairway on the beach. As if possessed, she began to sing at the top of her voice.

"Each night before you go to bed, my baby, whisper a little prayer for me . . . And tell all the stars above, this is dedicated to the one I love . . ." she sang out, rang out her message to the dark, still night. She knew that, wherever Comanche was, he could hear her, because any and everyone could hear her within a half mile radius. As she continued to sing her heart out, she began to walk away.

"While I'm away from you, my baby, I know it's hard for you. Because it's hard for me, and the darkest hour is just before dawn . . ."

As India got further and further from the beach, she thought about J.C. and his brethren, about his excellency and his superior power. And she walked, as if compelled by some unseen force. She walked as if she were treading the Cherokee Trail of Tears.

Chapter Eleven

Therefore said I, look away from me; I will weep bitterly,
Labor not to comfort me, because of the spoiling of the
daughter of my people.

Isaiah 22:4

When India finally stopped walking, several days later, miraculously she found herself in San Diego, amid a sea of people who were totally unaware of her and her unfortunate circumstances. She sat down at a harbor nearby, dazed and dismayed at her feat of having wandered over a hundred miles aimlessly.

After resting awhile, she arose and drifted to a nearby Denny's restaurant. She stood outside and attempted to sell a silver bracelet she had worn for years. Soon, a middle age man exited the establishment, picking his teeth with a tooth pick.

"Sir, would you like to buy this beautiful bracelet for ten dollars?" India asked timidly.

He reached into his pocket and extracted his wallet and gave India a ten dollar bill.

"You're forgetting the bracelet," India cried, as the man stated to walk away.

"You keep it," he instructed her.

"You can give it to your wife," offered India.

"Honey, my wife died ten years ago."

The perfect stranger smiled, and walked away. India went inside the restaurant and was seated by a waitress. She looked over the menu and decided on the Never Ending Shrimp.

After the waitress had served her three heaping helpings, and she could eat no more, she paid her bill, and was about to leave when she spotted a telephone next to the restrooms. She went over to the phone and placed a collect call to her mother, with whom she hadn't spoken to in several weeks. She was relieved when her mother accepted the call, and was genuinely glad to hear her voice.

She related to her mother that she was alone and desolate in San Diego. And then she felt what little strength she had retained escape her when her mother informed her that Angel had been moved yet again.

Her mother ordered her to stay there at the restaurant, saying that she would get her help without delay. India hung up the phone and sat down in the waiting area near the front door. She had no idea how much time had passed before a policeman entered and asked her name. Her mother, who was a reserve police officer with the Los Angeles Police Department, had pulled some strings in order to procure assistance from the San Diego Police.

India gazed up at the office. "My name is India," she told the officer. "Hello India, I'm Officer Agee. Your mother has wired you some money, and arranged for me to take you to the Western Union," he replied.

"Pleased to meet you," India acknowledged.

"My pleasure," bid Officer Agee, with a nod, as they walked to the patrol car and India scooted into the back seat.

"You must really have a wonderful mother to go to such lengths to help you," he surmised.

India laughed as she fumbled with the seatbelt, and though to herself how absurd his assumption was.

When they arrived at the Western Union office, India was soon handed three hundred dollars in cash. She was shocked at her mother's generosity. The officer then transported her to a charming motel and secured a room for her for two nights, as India had no identification. Then he shook her hand and wished her well after handing her the key to her room. Once in the exquisite room, India crawled into the queen side bed and curled up as if she were in a cocoon. She slept all night, and most of the next day.

When she awoke she thought of Angel, who was now seemingly lost in a cold, cruel system. India didn't know how she was going to rescue her baby from the systematic beast which had devoured her.

She reached for the phone at her bedside and called her mother to thank her for the money, and tell her that she was safe and warm, but far from tranquil, due to the state of her only child, whom she had not seen since she was six weeks old. And Angel had just turned two. In her two years of life, she had been dragged from place to place. As soon as she began to establish any sense of tranquility, she was brutally uprooted and moved again. She had never seen her father and had no recollection of her mother. And she was just an innocent child. What had been her transgression, that she should endure such suffering? She was merely a victim of circumstance, having been born to a mother who didn't have a home.

India began to weep over the phone, and could not refrain. Then, suddenly, she was silenced when she heard her mother say, "Okay, I'm going to get custody of my granddaughter."

"You should have gotten her long ago!" India scolded.

When India hung up the phone, she felt a glimmer of hope. Inspired, she arose and took a shower. After getting dressed, she walked out onto the streets of downtown San Diego, peering into the various shops.

She thought, "What if she and Bernard could get back together and make a happy home for their daughter." On an impulse, India walked into a tattoo parlor, and paid twenty dollars, of the money her mother had wired her, to have Bernard's name tattooed on her left breast, over her heart. Then, she walked around the downtown area, and handed dollar bills out to the transients there before returning to her hotel room.

The following day she checked out of the motel feeling refreshed, and went to the Greyhound Bus Station and bought a ticket to Los Angeles with her last fifteen dollars. It was a short, but pleasant trip, and she arrived with a sense of guarded confidence.

India found a safe haven at the nearby Sunlight Mission Church. Although she and her mother were gaining ground at forging a healthy relationship, it was still out of the question to think that they could dwell together in harmony. But she phoned her mother each day from the Mission as they united in a pact to reconcile Angel with her family.

India had relinquished her parental rights after she had been falsely assured that Angel was going to be adopted, as an infant. If she could not attain custody, then the next best thing was for her mother to rear her. After all, she was the only constant force in Angel's life, having followed her from home to home in an effort to try to provide her with some inkling of security.

At the Mission, India would complete her assigned chores, and then go to the neighborhood park and spend her days socializing and amusing herself with the people she met here, along with one or two of her fellow lodgers at the Mission. On Sunday, they held a church service led by the founder of Sunlight Mission Church, who was an ordained minister. At night, they would sleep on cots in a large, open area of the sanctuary.

About a week before India was due to get her SSI check, which would arrive at her mother's address, she purchased a local newspaper and turned to the section that listed apartments for rent. One ad nearly leaped out at her. It was for a furnished room in San Pedro, with utilities paid, and it was within her prospective budget. She called about it immediately, and told the owner that she would take it, sight unseen. It never occurred to her that he might want to screen his prospective tenant, and India arranged to meet him at the apartment building on the second day of the following month.

So, on the first of November, when India's check arrived at her mother's house, she immediately mailed it to India at the mission. India received it the following day, cashed it, and gave a donation to the mission before departing. She had arranged to pay one of the residents, who had a car, the take her to her new home.

India arrived there on time with only a bag of clothes which she had gotten at a clothing drive at the church. She sat down on the front porch, and waited for the owner to appear. He pulled up in a new Mercedes within a few minutes, got out of the car, and approached India with his right hand extended.

"Nice place," she smiled, shaking his hand.

"Thank you, I think you'll be very comfortable here," he replied.

After introducing themselves, he showed India to the apartment. It was more like a room, and the bathroom, which she would have to share was at the end of the hall. But it was nice, and clean, not to mention, affordable.

India completed the application, and paid her first month's rent, plus a small security deposit to her new landlord, and he presented her with the key. After he left, India went to a pay phone outside of the convenience store next door, and called her mother.

"I'm in!" she exclaimed.

Her mother's joy sounded sincere.

India decided to explore her new neighborhood. There was a Laundromat adjacent to the convenience store. She continued on for a few blocks and discovered that she was merely three short blocks from Ports O' Call. And there was a small park, just a block and a half from her place, where she sat and watched the rustic ships arrive and depart from the harbor. The aqua water glistened in the sunlight. India sat there, still, for an undeterminable amount of time, and watched the mystic, splendid sunset. She was home. This was most definitely a place where she could heal. As she sauntered back to her place, she was almost skipping by the time she got there. There was a gentle, sea breeze blowing the Autumn leaves around, and, all at once, India felt composed, and requited for all of the agony which she had almost grown accustomed to.

India became fast friends with her new neighbors, and they would wile away hours, sitting on the front stoop, talking and laughing. They shared what they had with one another, everything from cigarettes, to food. India would cook and deliver plates of food to Mike, a young guy who lived across the hall, and Bill, an older man who had no formal education, but was quite well-read and loved sharing his wealth of knowledge.

Most of the tenants were either existing on SSI or Social Security checks. They would borrow money from each other when one of them would run low on funds, and always paid each other back promptly on check day. The landlord would come on the first of each month to collect the rent. He was also good natured and cordial, always taking time to shoot the breeze with his householders. India was happy there, and flourishing, but she still longed for the child she'd never been afforded the opportunity to even get to know. Her intense longing for Angel was like a bottomless abyss which nothing and no one else could ever begin to fill. She felt completely incomplete.

Chapter Twelve

I have forsaken mine house, I have left mine heritage;
I have given the dearly beloved of my soul into the hand of her enemies.
Jeremiah 12:7

By the time India's mother, whom Angel called "Na Na," gained custody of Angel, she had been in and out of five different foster homes. At the tender age of three and a half, she had never known the familiarity that comes from having a real home. India thought about how traumatized and terrified Angel must have been each time she awoke in a foreign environment, and had no earthly idea where she was. Greeted by well meaning strangers and wondering why she was being forced to live out this cruel parody of life.

India had a vague indication of how her baby girl must have felt because she, herself, had experienced that sense of complete and total obscurity when she would awake in a remote room of a mental ward, not knowing where she was.

But now that Angel was with her Na Na, hopefully, she would lose the sense of being lost and dejected, and, eventually develop into a secure, confident, and stable child. After all, that was her birthright.

India felt her burden lightened now that Angel was closer to being where she had always belonged. She would go to the park, overlooking the harbor, daily. There, she would meditate and converse with God in the spirit. It was there that she decided to take a vow of celibacy, and dedicate her future to being reunited with her only child. She had a lot to be thankful for. She had literally been taken by the hand, and led by love.

Bernard was, undisputedly, the love of her life, having imparted to her, her true and profound yearning for a child. Their ten years together had been insatiable until the living, breathing, token of their unspoken covenant had manifested.

Then God had smiled down upon her when she'd found unlimited love and laughter with Danny in her sojourn to Georgia, where her soul had found peace, and her heart, a home. Then, after being led by the spirit back to California, she'd abode in the secret place with J.C., her savior, under the shadow of the Almighty. She had definitely known love, timeless and unswerving. And it had brought her through seemingly insurmountable circumstances. But now, she felt that she had come full circle. She felt in perfect tune with the universe. God had been her sure refuge, having enveloped her with His tender mercies and protective salvation. She knew that she was truly beloved of God, and she felt one with His still, infinite power. And she was certain that He would sustain her, and lead her to her undeniable destiny. Most people are lucky if they find one soul mate. India had been blessed to find three. Her life was definitely taking a turn for the better, and the future loomed bright.

One Sunday, after India had been settled in her place for about a month, her mother brought Angel to spend the day with her. Pop drove them in his van. Momma had passed away from cancer while India was in Georgia.

When India slid open the van door to reveal her baby, smiling broadly, her heart melted.

"Is this my big girl?" India beamed, as she gathered Angel in her arms.

They went to Ports O' Call and went on the boat ride around the harbor. India and Angel quickly bonded and India felt pure ecstasy each time Angel called her "Mommy." They had spoken several times over the phone, but now, the dream of being with her child, whom her empty arms had so longed for, was a reality. They had dinner at a seafood restaurant before they dropped India back at her place, and headed for him.

India sat on the porch and wallowed in the afterglow, recounting every moment of their blissful day together. She finally entered her apartment and fell to her knees before retiring, thanking and praising God for bringing the reunion to pass, after three long years. At long last

Angel was able to put a face with whom she had imagined "Mommy," to be. From that day forth, they spoke on the phone almost daily, and India would even go to spend the weekend about once a month. She had to catch three buses to get from San Pedro to Altadena. Sometimes, Angel and Na Na would meet her at the bus stop in downtown Pasadena. When Angel spotted her, she would run and jump in India's waiting arms, squealing with joy.

India made the most of her time with Angel. They would catch the bus to the mall, where India would indulge Angel at the toy store. She loved Barbie, and had quite a collection of them, both Black and White. She would play with them for hours in the bathtub before calling to India that she was ready for her to bathe her, dry her off, and put on her pajamas. Consequently, there were usually a medley of naked Barbie dolls strewn everywhere. India would make clothes for them, much to Angel's delight.

Angel was quite satisfied with the status quo, and felt that it was completely normal that she resided with her Na Na. She even suggested that India have her a baby brother, and give him to her and Na Na.

India's brother, Craig had divorced his wife, and he also lived with Angel and Na Na, along with his ten year old son. Craig served as a father figure for Angel, taking her to church on Sundays, and picking her up from preschool everyday.

It wasn't until Angel entered kindergarten that she came to the realization that most children lived with their mother and father, and began to question India. Her burning inquiry was, "Where is my daddy?" And, quite frankly, India had no idea. Bernard's family had moved from where they resided, around the corner, and India did not even know where to begin to look for him. But he promised Angel that she would try to find him.

Once, wanting to give Angel something concrete to cling to, she took her around the corner and showed her the house where Bernard had resided. Angel was in total awe, India showed her the back house, where she had been conceived and said, "This is where your daddy and I made you."

Angel pondered that notion, and went home and later confided in her Na Na that she was made in a barn. Needless to say, Na Na was not happy, and chastised India for her indiscretion.

India desperately wanted to find Bernard. Not for herself, but for Angel, at least that's what she told herself. Angel was perplexed as to why her father was not a part of her life.

One night, India picked up the telephone book and found Bernard's father listed in a neighboring city. It took all the courage she had to muster up the gumption to dial his number. When he answered, India said, "Hello, this is India."

"India?"

"Yes, Bernard's India" she explained.

"Oh, yes." They spoke with guarded curiosity.

Charlie, Bernard's father did not even know that Bernard had a child. India surmised that he had been too ashamed to inform his parents that they were estranged, and he had never even laid eyes on his daughter.

India inquired about Bernard's whereabouts, and Charlie reluctantly revealed that Bernard had moved up north with his mother and most of his siblings after he and his wife's divorce.

When India pressed, he related that Bernard lived in Sacramento, California. India nearly forgot to say, "Goodbye." She thanked Charlie, and immediately called information in Sacramento. When the information operator gave India the number, she hesitated, with her finger pressed down on the phone, frozen with a foreboding apprehension.

After a few minutes, she dialed the number. A woman answered. "Hello," she said in a voice that sounded, strangely, like India's. "May I speak to Bernard?" India asked.

"Who is this?" the woman demanded.

"This is his daughter's mother, who is this?" India inquired timidly.

"This is his wife!" the woman asserted.

India was shaken. She could not imagine Bernard ever being married to anyone except her.

"Oh, I'm sorry," India atoned. "I just wanted to arrange for him and his daughter to talk."

"I'm sure he would like that," the woman offered condescendingly.

India hung up the phone without leaving her number. She felt a teardrop burn her cheek as it traveled from the corner of her eye, down to her chin, and fell onto her chest, just above her broken heart.

Chapter Thirteen

In that day, saith the Lord, will I assemble her that halteth,
and I will gather her that is driven out, and her that I have afflicted.
Micah 4:6

Angel was seven years old when India decided to move to Altadena to be closer to her.

After a relentless search, India found the perfect place, a studio apartment which she had passed by countless times. It was clean. It was manageable, financially. And it was about half a mile from her mother's house.

Her mother helped her with the first month's rent, and security deposit, and India promised to faithfully repay her a little each month. They went to the Salvation Army, and found a twin bed, and a set of matching dressers, tables, and a desk. They also got a used refrigerator in good condition. The apartment came with a stove.

India bid farewell to all of her faithful friends in San Pedro, and moved in her new place with great expectations. Her new neighbors were mostly Hispanic and just as pleasant and friendly as they could be. She became acquainted with the manager and his wife, a Hispanic couple with three gorgeous children.

Being as she was so close to her mother's house, she would walk over there almost every day. And she and Angel soon formed a closeness that they had not possessed before. India spent most weekends with Angel, and they would have the best time together. Angel loved to comb India's hair in the most wild and outlandish styles. And India would polish Angel's fingernails. They would play board games. Angel's favorite was LIFE, and she would beg India to play again, and again for hours on end. India taught Angel to play Checkers, but, because she would cry when she lost, India would usually let India win.

Craig had remarried so he and his son no longer resided at the house. His new wife owned a dry cleaners, and they were quite prosperous, working together as a unified team. She had two sons from a previous marriage. And they all merged to form a vivacious family. India was elated that her brother had been fortunate enough to finally find true love.

They had all traveled to Las Vegas for the wedding, at which, Angel had served as the flower girl, adorned in the most lovely satin dress.

And Lillian, Craig's new wife, was beautiful, both inside and out. She fondly referred to India as "Sis." And she prophetically, became the sister that India never had.

India's relationship with her mother was notably improved, but still far from ideal. And, after about a year India was informed that her mother felt that it would be better if she not spend weekends with Angel. India felt that her mother had grown increasingly jealous over the unshakeable bond which she had cultivated with Angel, although her Mother gave no reason for her decision.

Instead, she sat Angel down and gingerly told her that she would not be spending the entire weekend with her anymore, but she would come over every day, adding that if Angel ever needed her for any reason whatsoever, all she need do is call, and she would be right there. Angel seemed okay with the new arrangements. She was so resilient, able to rebound from impossible obstacles. And, since she and India had been restored to one another, she had thrived into a delightful, exuberant eight year old, who excelled in school, and took life as it came.

However, the past which she had endured had left its invisible scars on her psyche. Her personality reminded India of the drama faces, as she was usually ecstatic, but sometimes experiences undeniable sorrow. During these times, she would cry and wail unrelentingly. She was, what was termed in Georgia as "tenderhearted."

Angel had forbore one of these crying spells after India had informed her that her father was married and miles away. After that, she never mentioned him. But India knew that she had internalized her deep and dismal feelings of rejection and hurt. And that these emotion were eating away at her chance of being whole and complete. She was already diminished and deprived because of the fact that she had never met her father and didn't even possess a picture of him. But India was hopeful and optimistic that father and daughter would one day be united.

As Angel grew in body and spirit, India began to wonder if, perhaps her little girl was her dearly departed Grandma, reincarnated. Especially after Angel had several dreams about an older woman who Angel thought was haunting her. It frightened her until she described the woman to India. India then showed Angel a picture of her great grandmother and Angel exclaimed, "That's her, mommy! That's the woman in my dreams."

In one particular dream, Grandma was begging Angel not to leave her. India was reminded of the time when Grandma was in the hospital, shortly before she died, and they were going to transport her to a convalescent home. Grandma had begged India to stay with her, but India had to leave because her mother, who had walked out of the hospital room, would have left her. India had always been plagued with guilt feelings about the incident, particularly since Grandma had passed away only a few short weeks later.

India reassured Angel, and convinced her that Grandma was merely visiting her, and that she was her guardian angel. She told her of how Grandma had foretold of Angel's birth, saying, "Talk about a pretty baby!" Angel smiled, consoled, and returned to her playful activities.

Then, there was the time that India could not reach Billie, who had been a dear friend of Grandma's on the phone. Billie lived directly across the street from Grandma's old house.

When India decided to go check on Billie, Angel insisted that she wanted to go with her. As soon as India turned onto the street, Angel excitedly announced, "I've been on this street before!"

"Oh, yes?" India replied, at first undaunted.

But it was when India approached Billie's house and Angel declared, "Billie lives right there," that she was moved with awesome wonder. She knew that Angel had never been to Billie's house, and there was no earthly way that she could have known where Billie lives, or even who Billie was. But then, she exclaimed,

"And that was Grandma's house!" pointing across the street.

India's mouth flew open. She was astounded.

"How did you know that?" she asked.

"I told you I've been on this street, Mommy," Angel replied unfazed.

"Where, in a dream?" India implored.

But Angel didn't answer. She instead, exited the car, and skipped up to the gate like she'd been there countless times. There were two houses on Billie's lot, and Angel marched right up to Angel's threshold.

When Billie came to the door, after a few minutes, Angel looked up at her and smiled a toothless grin. Billie returned the smile, delighted to see India with Grandma's great granddaughter, whom she met for the first time.

"Come in." she beckoned.

"We can't stay, I just wanted to check on you because I've been trying to call you," India explained.

"I was catching up on my sleep. I couldn't rest well last night," offered Billie, "So this is Angel!"

"Hi Billie!" quipped Angel.

"Well, well, we finally meet. Aren't you a pretty little lady," beamed Billie.

"We'll come back to visit when we can stay longer," interrupted India, still astonished by Angel's bizarre premonition.

India did not think it was the least bit improbable that her beloved daughter could have inherited her beloved grandmother's spirit. Quite the contrary, she believed that her grandmother had loved and adored her so intensely, that such a profound love could not have merely ceased to be, upon her demise. She became more and more convinced that some sort of magical quickening occurred upon Angel's conception in her womb. That Grandma's essence was transformed into what was now her blessed offspring.

And now, it was unmistakably evident that Angel's love and adoration for India was just as deep and enduring as the divine love which had preceded her existence.

Angel doted on her mother, and when they were together, they were wholeheartedly satisfied.

And in return, India lavished her affections on Angel. Although they did not live together, she managed to spoil her rotten. She did not have much money, but, with the little she had, she catered to Angel's every fancy, oftentimes sacrificing, and doing without things for herself.

Angel's happiness was India's number one priority in life, and she wished for the day that they could dwell together in a place of dreams.

Chapter Fourteen

And thine ears shall hear a word behind thee, saying. This is the way, walk ye in it, when ye turn to the right hand, and when ye turn to the left.

Isaiah 30:21

When Angel was ten years old, she began to have a recurring dream about Bernard. At first, she said nothing, but, when they persisted, she told India that she kept dreaming of her father in the clouds.

Although Angel had never laid eyes on Bernard, he had somehow manifested his presence unto her. Knowing that Angel had exhibited powerful spiritual qualities, India decided to call Charlie, Bernard's father. She was almost relieved, when he didn't answer the phone, and she left a message on his machine, saying that she had just called because she was thinking about Bernard, and wanted to relay Charlie to relay birthday wishes to him. Bernard's birthday was merely a few days away. She left her mother's phone number.

The following day, India received a call from Tony, Bernard's brother, informing her that Bernard had passed away a few weeks prior. He said that he and his dad had just that day returned from Sacramento, where they had buried Bernard. India tried to relay Angel's premonition of her father in the clouds to him, but realizing that she must have sounded deluded, she stopped herself, and asked, "What happened?"

"I don't know," answered Tony. "His apartment manager found him on the floor of his apartment."

India immediately surmised that Bernard had finally succumbed to the drugs.

Tony inquired about Angel.

"She's fine," India assured him. "But I don't know how she's going to take this."

By the time India hung up the phone, Angel was standing in front of her, asking what was wrong.

"That was your Uncle Tony," began India. "You've been dreaming about your father in the clouds because he passed away."

Angel exploded in a flood of tears, and she began to wail. Her Na Na rushed in to see what was all the commotion and Angel gasped, "My father died."

They both fell onto the bed and began to roll back and forth in insufferable grief. After what seemed like hours of anguished moaning, Angel grew silent.

But India knew in her heart that her child, at such a tender age, would never be consoled. She attempted to offer her solace, but she had to recognize the fact that Angel would never overcome. She could no longer daydream that she and her idealized father would one day be together. The dream had died with him.

In the weeks that followed, India searched for the illusive answers to why the love of her life had been stolen away at the age of thirty eight. She called Bernard's sister, Pauline, in Sacramento, and told her how Angel was totally consumed with grief, and that she didn't even have a picture of her father.

Pauline told India that she remembered her, and that Bernard had confided in her that he had a child. She promised to send an obituary.

During the course of their conversation, India mentioned something about Bernard's wife to which Pauline replied, "I don't know what they told you, but Bernard did not have a wife."

India was aghast. She told Pauline how she had attempted to reach Bernard, only to be discouraged by the woman who answered his phone, and identified herself as his wife. "Bernard was never married," reiterated Pauline with conviction. There was anger in her voice. But it could not compare with the fury which India felt. She was furious to know that Bernard's wanna be wife had lied to her, and literally changed the path of all of their lives forever. She would never have faltered in pursuing Bernard, so that their daughter could have seen his substance and become acquainted with his way, and apprehended his love.

Pauline also assured India that Bernard did not have any other children. India felt relieved, but cheated. She had been deceived out of her divine providence. Angel had been heartbroken after India had told her that her father was married. And it was all because of one contemptible lie.

When India reported to Angel that her father was never remarried and had no other children, she seemed pacified, as if some of the staggering weight that she was bearing had been lifted off her shoulders.

But about six months after Bernard's death, the strangest thing happened. Angel began to have pain in her legs. It worsened over the following weeks, until Angel was unable to walk. India and her mother took her to doctor after doctor who tested her for everything from pediatric arthritis to sickle cell anemia, but found nothing wrong. After about a month, the pain subsided, and eventually disappeared completely.

Na Na thought it was a good idea to seek counseling for Angel, in order for her to get help in dealing with her father's death, and the fact that she would never get the opportunity to know his undeniable similarities with her. It was during these intense sessions that the fact painfully emerged that Angel had subconsciously hated her father for not being present in her life. It was unearthed that this hatred had turned to a piercing guilt, which gnawed at her psyche, causing her mental as well as physical anguish.

When India learned this she then knew just how deeply her child's torment ran, even to the depth of her soul. Although India felt that Angel's wound was incurable, she attempted to do everything within her power to ease her sorrow. She lavished her with love and attention, and tried to instill a sense of belonging in her, but the bottomless pit of her profound loss still consumed her.

The family counseling also enabled India to finally comprehend the origin of her mother's profound disdain toward her. She had always suspected that it was because she was the spitting image of her father, whom her mother had divorced when India was three years old. But, it was revealed during an intense counseling session that her mother had also obtained a restraining order against India's father, just as she had secured against her during her trial of homelessness.

Her mother also alleged that she had divorced her father because of his adamant refusal to help her financially. So India finally rationalized the motive behind her mother's insistence that she give her a generous portion of any money she'd ever received. It was her mother's way of affecting her vengeance, in making the child pay for the sins of the father.

Once India grasped these ideas, at least she had a concept of why her mother had hated her. Although it was something far beyond her control, and, in view of the fact that her father had died four years after the divorce, she at least now possessed a concrete reason, howbeit far from a remedy. However illogical and inexcusable it was, like Angel, she now had a comprehensible confirmation for her anguish.

However, after a few more months passed, Angel's mourning was unexpectedly transformed into joy when she was an uninvited guest at a candle party that she attended while visiting a friend and her aunt. Angel had no idea that the hostess of the candle party was her Uncle Tony's ex-wife, Anna, whom she had never met.

Angel was sitting in the living room, slightly bored, when Anna came up to her and sat down beside her, inching closer and closer, until she was staring Angel square in the face.

"Who are your parents?" inquired Anna.

"India and Bernard," answered Angel, bewildered.

"Bernard who?" exclaimed Anna.

"Bernard Clay," replied Angel.

"Aja! Aja!" yelled Anna, beckoning to her daughter, who was in another room. Angel didn't know what to think. She feared for a moment that they were going to jump her.

Just then, Aja emerged from her room.

"This is your cousin!" exclaimed Anna. "Your Uncle Bernard's daughter!" At first, Angel was perplexed. But then Anna explained to her that Aja was her father's brother's daughter, and that she was among a houseful of Clays.

Angel's bewilderment turned to delight at the joyous reunion. By the time she came home to report the encounter to India, she was giddy with jubilation.

"Guess who I met?" she squealed.

"Who?" India probed.

As Angel gleefully recounted her evening, India's spirits lifted. It inspired her to see Angel this happy at her homecoming, of sorts, and felt that there was hope that the breach could be healed.

Angel's entire mood and outlook lightened. She had finally discovered roots from her paternal lineage, which had, before, been only an obscure mystery.

Angel visited Anna and her cousins, Aja and Anthony on several special occasions, following their initial encounter. This led to a chain of events that familiarized her with her father's people, including her grandfather.

After it got back to Charlie that Bernard's daughter had connected with her cousins, and about the kinship that was so obvious between them he wanted to meet Angel. Especially after learning that she was the mirror image of Bernard. It was true. She possessed all of his mannerisms. She talked like him, she laughed like him, she personified him in an unconscious, yet uncanny fashion.

So Charlie arranged to take Angel out to dinner along with Tony and his current wife, their son, and Aja and Anthony. So, one Saturday, Aja came and picked up Angel, and drove her to Tony's house. There, the family gathered. Charlie looked Angel up and down and saw for himself that she, indeed, was the living likeness of Bernard. He wiped away a tear from his eye before embracing her in a bear hug.

They dined at a buffet dinner at a restaurant near Tony's house, but Angel could not eat. She was consumed with the tangible reality of being surrounded by her father's flesh and blood, her very own kindred.

"You ain't got nothing on your plate but a beef rib," scolded Charlie, "There ain't no meat on the bones." Angel merely chuckled, as Anthony flirted with the waitress. She felt an undeniable oneness with this clan. She could look in their faces and see herself reflected back.

After that momentous evening, India wanted to cultivate the relationship which Angel had established with her family. She called Charlie and invited him to dinner, and he gladly accepted. She got Pop to barbeque a slab of ribs and some chicken thighs. And she prepared a potato salad, a green salad, and baked beans. For dessert, she made a peach cobbler, and bought some vanilla ice cream to top it off.

The ribs were tough, and Charlie made no effort to conceal the fact that in his expert opinion, Pop did not know how to properly barbeque ribs. "It's all in the marinade," he explained. "You have to start with the sauce, the water, and the vinegar. I can't even eat this meat," Charlie grumbled, as he, India and Angel sat around the dining room table at Na Na's house, laughing and chatting.

Charlie ate everything else, except the ribs, and raved about the peach cobbler. But he repeated over and over his disappointment with the ribs, expounding on his recipe for the sauce, the water and the vinegar. Angel kept India in stitches for weeks afterward, mimicking him.

A few weeks after the dinner, Charlie stopped by unexpectantly, and Angel was not at home. But he gave India the most extraordinary gift to give to her. It was a guardian angel necklace, surrounded by what looked like diamonds, but were probably, in all actuality, a realistic looking cubic Zirconium.

When Angel came home, India told her that her grandpa had come to see her, and left a gift. And, when she opened the box, revealing the necklace, she radiated with sheer delight.

India felt, in her heart of hearts, that they had come full circle. Although Angel was never afforded the opportunity to know her father, she gained a rare sense of him through his father and brother, and she cherished each unifying experience, and engraved it into her mind and heart.

Charlie had also revealed to India how Bernard died. It wasn't drugs after all, as India had assumed. But he had undergone an operation whereby half of his pancreas was removed. As a result, he'd developed diabetes, but refused to properly take his insulin injections.

One fateful day, when he was alone in his apartment, he'd fallen and hit his head after going into a diabetic coma. His landlord found him, but it was too late.

India couldn't help but wonder that, if only it had not been for the dreadful life told to her by his girlfriend, that per chance she and Bernard could have found their way back to each other. And maybe he would still be alive, because India would have insisted that he take his insulin. But fate had dealt its hand.

Chapter Fifteen

The Lord thy God in the midst of thee is mighty; He will save,
He will rejoice over thee
with joy; He will rest in His love, He will joy over thee with singing.
Zephaniah 3:17

Although India spent the larger part of her time with Angel, over her mother's house, she still retained and maintained her apartment nearby. It was there that she spent quiet time alone in meditation and worship with God, who had brought her thus far. He'd led her, and fed her from the days when her prayers pierced the heavens and came unto His ears. And she'd found significant favor with God, who lavished her with bountiful blessings above measure. Even to the extent of manifesting manifold miracles toward her.

When India was home, she lived a life of prayer and piety. And, although she resided by herself, it became most evident that she was not alone.

India began to notice that her bed would gently rock back and forth as she lay perfectly still. This didn't frighten her however. To the contrary, it gave her great comfort as she gave to the realization that she was resting in the bosom of her dearly departed Grandma whom she'd always known was with her still.

Another supernatural manifestation occurred after India placed a beautiful bookmark, which she had found one day coming from placing roses on her Grandma's grave, on her wall. She hung it from a tack suspended on a string, next to her T.V. Then, that evening, she noticed that the bookmark had turned all the way around, in and of itself. The back of it was facing her as he stood before it, dumbfounded.

This began to happen rather frequently, about once or twice a week, until India was convinced that it had to be the workings of an angel. She was sure that it was Bernard. And each time this transpired, she was overcome with sheer joy. She would begin to sing and would turn off her T.V. and begin to pray, thanking God that he found her worthy enough to dwell with His holy angels.

India told no one of these occurrences, but simply rejoiced in the knowledge that the secret of God was upon her tabernacle, and that His holy spirit dwelt with her and in her. She felt wholly holy in this sanctified heirship.

India resided in her apartment for seven years and continued to behold these magnificent wonders, abiding in awe and adoration.

One day, she was over her mother's house delighting in Angel, just amusing herself in her lovely daughter. India was sitting on the couch in the living room, and Angel was in the adjacent room, when seemingly, from out of no place, a beautiful rainbow appeared in the dining room, when seemingly, from out of no place, a beautiful rainbow appeared in the dining room. It went from one wall, across the ceiling, and down the opposite wall, forming an arc over Angel.

India gazed at it in total and complete fascination, but Angel took it in stride.

"Look at the pretty rainbow," she noted.

"It's a sign," explained India, "Rainbows are a symbol of God's covenant."

It indeed was a mystical omen, which had never been displayed either before or since. And it was a foreshadowing of God's ordained promise to their certain future. He had ordered their steps.

Angel's relationship with Na Na grew into one which was tumultuous and troubled when she became a teenager. She would often call India in tears, and India would have to mediate.

India feared that her mother would attempt to mistreat Angel the same way in which she had abused her. One afternoon, after one of their arguments, India was sitting next to Angel on the couch, stroking her hair as she lie, wrapped in a blanket.

"Will you move in?" Angel asked in a still, small voice.

India informed her that she had just written a letter to Na Na, suggesting that she move in with them. With that, Angel closed her eyes, and fell asleep.

Angel had just turned fifteen years old when India moved in. Her mother's abominable pride would never allow her to admit she needed India. To the contrary, she made it seem like she was doing her a favor.

Although she had mellowed some in her old age, her evil nature was still quite evident. This contrasted greatly with India's sacred spirit, but she was determined to persevere for Angel's sake. She prayed that her devotion could overrule the darkness that reigned in her mother's heart.

With India there, Angel was happier than she'd ever been. And India's illusive dream of dwelling with her daughter had finally come true. They didn't always have to be engaging or talking with each other, they were content just being together.

India was glad that she was there for Angel when they received some bad news. Tony called India to notify her that Charlie had suffered a sudden heart attack and passed away. Angel took it hard, but was grateful that, at least she'd gotten to know him. She clung to the guardian angel necklace around her neck, and it took on an even more special and significant meaning. Charlie's wife, Estella, had died about a year or so after Bernard passed away, and she was buried beside him in Sacramento.

India attended Charlie's funeral, but Angel was not up to going. She had never been to a funeral, and she was still staggering from the loss. But India knew that Charlie had joined the assembly of angels who were guiding and guarding them. This knowledge endowed India with strength for the journey.

Although she paid her mother rent, India was treated like a live-in maid. But it was well worth it to be able to be there for Angel. India cooked and cleaned and washed clothes to no end. But each morning when Angel would sing, "Bye, Momma!" before leaving for school, her burden would turn to banter as she resounded,

"Bye sweetie, have a great day."

So the three generations dwelt together under one roof, experiencing the spectrum of all the varied shades of life. Angel continued to grown in spirit and in stature as Bernard's essence illuminated from her more and more in both her appearance and mannerisms. She definitely embodied his smile and style. And this is what fueled India with hope and vigor, coupled with the awareness that she was partaker of God's sacred anointing, ordained for such a time as this.

Her first pregnancy had tragically ended in miscarriage. And her second pregnancy had ended in a miscarriage of justice. But God, in his ultimate authority had executed judgment, and established order by setting things aright.

India was now convinced that indeed, *"All things work together for good to them that love God, to them that are the called, according to His purpose."* She had read it a thousand times, but, now, the infallible truth and relevance of the scripture enveloped her, as she rested in God's love.

But India was glad that the Bible did not instruct her to love her mother, but, rather, to honor her. And this, she did, taking into consideration that her mother was the matriarch of their family, and the only living grandparent that Angel had.

Yet, she held a thriving contempt for her mother, which grew from the fact that she failed to appreciate anything that India did, and shamefully took her for granted.

Once, when India complained about all she did in the house, her mother's callous response was,

"What do you do?"

India decided that her dear Grandma's philosophy, concerning her spiteful daughter was accurate when she'd stated, "Everybody born in March is crazy."

So, she was determined to bear her yolk without complaining, even though her mother had habits which drove her up the wall after she had lived alone for so many years.

One of which was her mother's silent refusal to rinse out the bathroom sink after washing her false teeth. Thus, leaving particles of food in the sink, for India to be forced to clean, although it literally turned her stomach. No matter how many times India asked her to please rinse out the sink, her mother simply shunned her pleas. India stopped asking her after her mother turned it around, and somehow made it all about her by saying that she was "obsessed."

But the irony was that India did love her mother, and they truly did celebrate some tender times together, especially around the holidays, when family is what really matters.

On Thanksgiving, she and her mother would prepare a bountiful feast together. And India would scrimp and save for months prior to Christmas in order to purchase extravagant gifts for her family. These were precious times, and India clung to the beloved memories of her family being together at last, no matter what the sacrifice had been.

Chapter Sixteen

Hear, O Heavens, and give ear, O earth: for the Lord hath spoken,
I have nourished
and brought up children, and they have rebelled against me.
Isaiah 1:2

Unlike her mother, India cherished the fact that her daughter was so much like her deceased father. But children learn what they live. And Angel was not the person that she would have been, had India reared her from birth. India's world was shaken when she was forced to come to the realization that her mother's negative influence had penetrated Angel's personality.

Angel was nearly seventeen years old when she began to rise up again India. Because her Na Na had never physically disciplined her, she had a reckless lack of respect for authority. India had warned her mother that this would happen when Angel was younger. But, she had dismissed the omens, saying that she knew what she was doing.

Angel was sharpened by her horrible beginning and by her Na Na's undeniable force on her character. They both possessed a massive pride which prevented them from admitting when they were wrong, no matter how abrasive the transgression. Once instance transpired after Angel had a girlfriend stay over one night. They had ordered pizza, and had quite a bit left over. So, for dinner the following evening India prepared beanies and weenies for Angel and heated up two slices of leftover pizza for herself. When Angel saw the pizza in the toaster oven, she proceeded to throw a fit, screaming and culminating in her asserting "I don't want you here, you schizophrenic freak . . . you schizophrenic freak!" Then she went into the living room and began to cry uncontrollably.

"What on earth is going on?" demanded Na Na.

I didn't think Angel would mind if I ate a few slices of her pizza because I had to throw out the last pizza she had after it stayed in the refrigerator too long," explained India.

At that point they smelled something burning. India rushed to the kitchen to find Angel burning a letter in the sink.

"What in the world are you doing?" charged India.

"Leave me alone! Leave me alone!" screamed Angel at the top of her lungs. She then grabbed a butcher knife from the sink, and raced past India into the living room and locked the door. Luckily Na Na was able to talk to her, and diffuse the situation. Things were calm for a while, but, a few months later, Angel had a horrific outburst. She had called a family meeting and became enraged, cussing up a storm. India got up and walked away saying, "I refuse to listen to this language."

"If you walk away . . ." Angel started.

By this time India was already in the kitchen. She re-entered the living room just as Angel began to rant and rave, jumping up in India's face, and hitting her fist in the palm of her hand. India was afraid, because she knew that, if Angel hit her, she would have knocked her through the floor. So she just went to her room. Angel followed her with her violent rampage. "My bitch ass mother doesn't do anything for me," she yelled in a deafening pitch.

India said nothing. She was more embarrassed than angry, knowing that their neighbors could hear. She didn't speak to Angel for several days, until one day, Angel was crying to Na Na that India was ignoring her. "Why don't you talk to her about it?" suggested Na Na. But, instead of apologizing, and trying to make amends, Angel began another tirade.

"I think you owe me an apology," prompted India.

"I don't owe you anything," barked Angel, "And, I want you to leave."

"I'm working on it," declared India.

"Not fast enough" hurled Angel.

She left the room briefly, then returned and demanded all of her pictures, saying, "I don't want you to have any memories of me." When she added, "If you give me my pictures, I'll never say another word to you," India conceded, and got down her photos albums from her closet. She began removing all of Angel's pictures. All the while, Angel was cussing up a blue streak.

"You bitch! You whore! You're going to end up all by yourself!" she declared.

"I'll never been alone because I have Jesus," India maintained.

"You have Jesus?" mocked Angel, "If you say another word, I'll punch you in the face."

"I have never disrespected my mother no matter how badly she treated me," pointed out India. "And I have been too good to you to talk to me that way."

"I want you to leave, and Na Na wants you to leave," asserted Angel.

"Na Na needs me," observed India.

"No she doesn't! When I asked her why you want to live where nobody wants you, she said 'I guess it's because she can't afford to live anywhere else for $250.00 a month!'" The words stung like a razor's edge piercing India's core.

She grabbed her purse and started for the door. Angel grabbed a picture of her and India, encased in a glass frame, and flung it to the floor, shattering it. India picked up the phone to call 911, and Angel pulled the cord out of the wall. India rushed out the front door, and went to a pay phone and called the police. Then she returned to the house and waited in the car until the officer arrived.

She led them into the house and showed him the broken glass, and the phone, pulled out of the wall. He went o Angel's room and talked to her and told her to leave her mother alone. Angel was crying, and she had cut herself on the glass. India grabbed her Bible, her purse, and her nightgown and went to a motel, which had been a safe haven when she was pregnant and homeless. Once inside the motel room, she thought about her Grandma. Her mind flashed back to when she was about eight years old, and her Grandma lived with them while babysitting her and her brother.

One morning, after her mother and grandmother had argued, her mother had told her, "I don't care where you go, just be out of my house by the time I get home." Grandma had tearfully found shelter elsewhere, as God was her unyielding refuge and strength, just as he had proved to be for India. Both she and her dearly departed Grandma were God fearing women who knew that they were both strangers and sojourners on the earth, just passing through on their way to their heavenly home.

And now, Angel proved to be in conformity with her grandmother, in the detestable manner in which they entreated their mothers. They were both unthankful and unholy. So India stayed in the motel room and read her Bible, and fasted and prayed. She always found solace in the Psalms, *if it had not been the Lord who was on our side . . .*

After two days, she felt relieved, and returned home. But she wondered how her daughter, whom she had virtually dedicated her life to, since returning to California, could mount up against her in such vain glory. She felt dismayed and dejected. She doubted that things would ever be the same between them. And she yearned for the little girl who had once filled her days with sparkling abundance, and her heart with pure rhapsody.

Chapter Seventeen

How can I myself alone bear your cumbrance,
and your burden, and your strife?
Deuteronomy 1:12

Shortly before Angel's eighteenth birthday, she left home and moved in with her boyfriend and his family. She was gone for six months, and, during that time, she rarely came to the house. She and her boyfriend, Tim, did spend her eighteenth birthday with India, who prepared a pot of spaghetti and garlic bread for them. She also got a chocolate sheet cake with whipped cream frosting along with strawberry ice cream. India had participated in a clinical trial, testing a new medication for people with her diagnosis, and had been compensated over $3,000.00. She spent a good part of it buying birthday gifts for Angel, and also gifted her with a substantial amount of cash.

They also spent Thanksgiving and Christmas with India. Na Na had gone over to Craig's to join in their festivities. India filled the house with love and food, and once again, showered Angel and Tim with gifts and money. Then, one day in February, Angel phoned Na Na and asked, "Do you love me and Tim?"

"Yes, of course," answered Na Na.

"Well, would you let us move into the garage?" Angel entreated.

Na Na explained that the garage was not fit for human occupancy, but divulged that they could move into Angel's room. She did not even bother to discuss it with India, who was opposed to the idea. For one thing, they were not married, and the idea of Angel shaking up with her boyfriend under her grandmother's roof just didn't seem proper or adequate. And also, India had thoroughly cleaned Angel's room during her absence, and had been horrified to find a gun in Angel's underwear drawer. It was the first time that she had handled a gun in her life before discarding it in the bottom of the garbage can, which had been emptied the following day. She shuddered to evoke what kind of nightmarish activities Angel could be involved in, and was dumbfounded at the notion that she could defile their sanctuary by bringing a gun into their home.

Na Na was aware of the incident, yet she accepted them moving in. So, Angel and Tim came over the next day to have a family meeting with India and Na Na. They explained how their stuff kept coming up missing at his place, and how they just needed to save some money and would get their own apartment by April. They agreed to help in the house.

India felt that she could tolerate anything for a mere two months, and, that Sunday, she went and got them, and brought them and their belongings to the house. At first, things were civil, and India went out of her way to tolerate the circumstances, in the belief that it was only transitional. She would lovingly prepare Sunday dinners and patiently having to wait to use the bathroom when it was occupied. But Angel and Tim totally dishonored their pact to help with the household chores, and India ended up cleaning up behind them. She absolutely abhorred having a twenty-one year old man in the house who would not even take out the trash or put the garbage cans out on the curb once a week. They proved to be just two more people to whom she was in servitude.

April came and went and, not only did they abandon the idea of moving, but they had both quit their jobs, and were living off of the fat of the land. India harbored her growing resentment for several months, giving places to offenses while remaining reserved, and restrained her utter indignation until July. Then, one night, she got up to check the doors, as she'd always done. When she saw that Angel and Tim had, once again, cooked and left their dirty dishes for her to have to wash, she seethed with anger which had been brewing for seven months. She wanted to sound off like a tea kettle that had reached its boiling point. But she thought better of that notion when she realized that it was past midnight. So instead, she sat down and wrote a letter to Angel and Tim, which was how she'd always best expressed herself. She told them how hurt and offended she was that they treated her like their personal servant, and reminded them of all their broken promises. She said that she couldn't comprehend how, although neither one of them was working, they refused to life a finder to do anything around the house, and she signed it "Disappointed Mom." She then retired to bed, but sleep eluded her that night.

India was in the shower when Angel got up and read the letter. She could hear her bewailing to Na Na. When India emerged from the bathroom and went to her room, Angel flung open her door and demanded that they meet in the living room for a family meeting. India dressed and went to the living room. As soon as she sat down, Angel began to probe her, "Who do you think you are?" she charged. It was as if their roles were reversed, and she was the authority figure, sitting in judgment, and India was the insolent child. She went on and on, spewing venom, and not allowing India to get a word in edgewise.

"This has been brewing for months and I haven't said anything because I don't like strife!" India shouted above Angel.

"Well you didn't do a very good job of holding it in," Angel countered. "You've been going around here moping for months, and you making everybody uncomfortable."

Then Na Na broke into the conversation saying, "Wait a minute, Angel, listen to this. She complains about me not flushing the toilet or rinsing out the sink!"

They both proceeded to gang up on India, hurling false indictments, and attempting to justify themselves, in their immoral and misguided sanctification. By the time Angel arose and stormed out of the room, India felt drained. She was repulsed by their shameful and hideous display, and she was bruised to the bone that her mother and her daughter would turn on her merely because she had complained about being perpetually persecuted by the two people whom she had blessed above measure.

Then she heard Angel recounting the meeting to Tim, who had remained in their room. "She can go! She can leave!" she jeered. It was like pouring the proverbial salt in the wound. India concluded that she would, indeed leave. She decided that she would allow them to live their neurotic lives together, without her bearing their misplaced reproach. She was not willing or able to endure it any longer.

That day, she purchased what she hoped would be her final, one-way ticket to Georgia. When she started the car, Ray Charles crooned over the radio, blowing *Georgia On My Mind;*

> *O, the arms that reach out to me.*
> *O, the eyes that smile tenderly.*
> *Still in peaceful dreams I see,*
> *The road leads back to you.*
> *O Georgia, Georgia, no peace, no peace I find,*
> *Just an old sweet song,*
> *Keeps Georgia on my mind.*

India took it for a definite sign.

India did not speak to Angel or her mother for days. After a while, she began to talk to her mother, but still said nothing to Angel. She knew right well that it was God's will for her to honor her mother, no matter what. But, the Bible made no provision for taking crap from your kids.

It seemed like an infinity until India boarded the Greyhound bus, bound for Columbus, Georgia, once more. She knew that she would probably never see her mother again. As she reclined in her seat, gazing out the window at the fleeting countryside, she thought that she may not know what her future holds, but she knows she holds her future.

Chapter Eighteen

To everything there is a season, and a time to every purpose under the heaven.
Ecclesiastes 3:1

When India stepped off the bus in Columbus three days later, at 5:00 A.M., she stepped from darkness into dawn, both literally and figuratively. It was a new beginning. She still believed that she possessed the sacred covenant, the promise of tomorrow. She claimed her baggage before calling a cab to transport her to the Motel 6. Once there, she showered and climbed into the bed and went to sleep immediately. When she awoke, it was around noon, and she felt invigorated. She decided to check out the trailer park where she used to live to see if they had any vacancies. She chose to walk there, and absorb all of the Southern splendor which she had so hungered for.

The thick growth of exalted trees hiding the trickling creeks and streams like a shroud, reminded India of what she had missed. When she arrived at the trailer park, which was about a country mile from the motel, she was surprised to find that most of the old trailers had been replaced with newer models. She went to the office and discovered that the previous owners were no longer there.

"Hello," India greeted the young man seated behind the counter.

"Hi, can I help you?" he quipped cheerfully.

"I used to live here years ago, and I've just returned to Columbus. Do you have any furnished trailers available?" India queried.

"Yes, certainly. I have a few I can show you" informed the young man as he motioned toward the door.

"My name is India. I lived here when the Irwins were the owners. You've really done wonders with the park," she declared.

"Yeah, I bought it from the Irwins 'bout eight years ago. By the way, I'm Archie," he clarified as they walked together. Archie showed India three vacant trailers. All three were appealing, but India chose an inviting two bedroom trailer that was close to the office, where they returned to execute the business of securing India's new residence.

When she shook hands with Archie and bid him farewell, she felt quickened within her spirit. She walked over a short distance to the adjacent trailer park, and knocked on Barbara's door. Barbara and India had kept in contact throughout her twelve year long sabbatical from Georgia. Barbara peeked through the lace curtain on the window in her door, and let out a shriek.

"India, is that really you?" she squealed as she flung open the door.

"It's me in the flesh," laughed India.

"You haven't changed a bit!" lied Barbara. "How long have you been back?"

"I just arrived this morning."

"Well, you get yourself in here. If you ain't a sight for sore eyes," Barbara prodded.

India unraveled the tale of how she had found her way back to Georgia. They exchanged tidings, and Barbara dished the scoop on all the locals before driving back to the Motel 6 to retrieve her bags. India dropped her belongings off at her new sanctuary. And, after giving Barbara a tour, she treated her to Captain D's, where they gorged themselves on catfish filets while yammering on, and amusing themselves until they were full.

India grew wistful when Barbara asked her whatever became of Danny. India spelled out how she and Danny had parted ways after being denied custody of Angel. Barbara dropped India off at home after making plans to spend the next day together shopping. It was Barbara's day off. She worked on the Army base at Fort Benning, and had been employed there for decades.

The next morning, the sun seemed to surge forth to welcome India. She and Barbara shopped 'til they dropped. They went to Kmart and Sears, where India purchased all of her household necessities, including a 20-inch television set. India had the finest time arranging and rearranging the décor and beautifying her new shrine. She spent the next few days tending to the business of establishing telephone and utility services. She also had to call the toll free number to Social Security to report her change of address. She felt so lucky that she could receive her benefits no matter where she moved in the United States.

Once settled, she wrote a letter to her mother, informing her that she was sage, and giving her mother her new telephone number. But, India would usually call them on Sundays. Angel's demeanor progressed gradually from bitterness to enlightenment. And their long distance relationship slowly developed into one that was loving and cordial again.

India felt compelled to start attending church. She chose Mount Zion Baptist Church, which wasn't far from her trailer park. She certainly wasn't seeking love, but love found her once again, in the form of a man by the name of Earl Nelson, one of her church members. He had approached her upon her first visit, after noticing that she was a newcomer, and seized the opportunity to make her acquaintance and initiate a friendship. They started attending the services together and soon began seeing each other socially. They reveled in each other's company. Earl was fine as an aged wine, and just as intoxicating, and India soon came to the conclusion that their meeting was neither accidental or incidental, but rather the hand of God.

Their mutual adoration transcended into agape love, the perfect unconditional love with God as its core. And, after a year of courting they found themselves making wedding plans. They were married at Mount Zion Baptist Church, where they had met, with the entire congregation in attendance. India was blissful. Angel and Na Na did not make the trip, but they were both overjoyed.

Earl was a real estate broker and owned several homes in the Columbus area. He and India moved into a beautiful brick house. It was India's dream house and she dwelt there with her dream man. They had not consummated their union until their wedding night, and India felt like a born again virgin.

The following morning, as her husband slept, she slipped away, and went and sat in the backyard, under a fig tree, to commune with God. As she sat in the lounge char, she closed her eyes to pray. When she opened her eyes, she looked, and, lo and behold, she saw what appeared to be rain drops, falling down from the cloudless sky. She went and stood in the holy place, and let God rain his divine blessings upon her. And, as she stood there in awe, she knew that she had finally come into her season of abundance, and she had been baptized in blessing. Her vague vision of perfect peace had been realized, and her innermost dreams were now yielding fruit.

So, herein lies India's solemn song of providence, even the former and latter rain. How Almighty God carried her from glory to glory in his steadfast faithfulness, to which there shall never be an ending.